THE
BLOSSOMING
UNIVERSE
OF Violet
Diamond

THE
BLOSSOMING
UNIVERSE
OF Violet
Diamond

brenda woods

SCHOLASTIC INC.

ISBN 978-0-545-83150-5

12 11 10 9 8 7 6 5 4 3 2   14 15 16 17 18 19/0

Printed in the U.S.A.   40

First Scholastic printing, December 2014

Design by Ryan Thomann
Text set in Minister Light
Chapter opener art courtesy of IZO/Shutterstock.com

In loving memory of my brother—
Arthur Preston Woods, Jr.

1

THE PUZZLING UNIVERSE OF VIOLET DIAMOND

Did you ever have a dream that's so good, you wish you could save it forever instead of having it go back to that place in your mind where dreams become quieter than whispers, quiet like snowflakes falling?

And it's such an awesome dream that makes you so happy that right after you wake up, you rush to write it down because you can't just let it evaporate into nothing?

Did you ever have a dream like that? Last night, I did.

In my dream I was walking along one of those picture-perfect beaches you see in vacation ads, where seals sunbathe on rocks and tropical fish swim in see-through-blue water. In the distance, dolphins leaped from the ocean, and even though it was daytime and the sun was shining bright, a crescent moon hung in the sky. My mom was on one side, my dad on the other, holding my hands. Daisy, my older sister, was walking ahead of us. In my dream we all looked alike, same skin, same hair, same big white teeth that gleam when we smile.

Barefoot people walked by us on the beach and smiled. Everyone could tell, just by looking at us, we were a family. There were no question marks in their eyes, no looks on their faces that remind me of puzzles with missing pieces, no under-the-microscope stares.

But the absolute best part of the dream was that my dad was there with us. I snuggled close to him, his arm hugged my shoulder, and he looked at me with love in his eyes.

And then, my alarm went off and I woke up. Outside, the rain was pouring and a nearby lightning strike lit my room like a camera flash.

I grabbed my 500-page journal where I write down words I've never heard before along with their definitions, lists of all sorts of things, and my wishes that never seem to come true. I read the first wish I'd ever written.

1. I Wish My Dad Was Alive Instead of Dead.

Somehow, my wish had found its way into my dream.

I flipped to some blank pages at the back, started a new section called *Dreams I Always Want to Remember,* and began scribbling down the dream. Suddenly, I stopped writing and thought about the dream at the beach, my dad holding my hand, the smile that was in his eyes. Father's Day, a day I sometimes wish didn't exist, was coming up. I could feel my dream happiness vanish and the sadness coming, and even though I tried hard not to let them, all at once the gloomy clouds from outside got sucked in through my ears and invaded my brain. Did you know violets actually shrink? They do, and I did.

2

A PREDICTABLE SUMMER
OF BORING NOTHING

Tomorrow was the last day of school before summer vacation, but my best friend, Athena, was leaving tonight for Greece, where her grandparents live in a house that overlooks the beach. Lucky for her but unlucky for me because it meant I'd have a whole summer without my best friend. It was no secret that I wished I was going with her.

A dead and dull summertime awaits me.

Lately, I'd been imagining all of the boring nothing I was going to fill the summer with. *If boredom was something you eat,* I wondered, *what would it taste like?* Maybe like chicken broth when you're sick, mashed potatoes without gravy, or macaroni minus the cheese.

The sky was blue and it was a little hot except under the

shade of trees. "My mom said I could have a cat this morning," I told Athena as we strolled along home from school.

Athena smiled. "She finally said yes?"

"Yep. She must have gotten tired of me begging all the time. She's going to take me to the shelter."

"A recycled pet?" Athena smiled again. There is one thing Athena Starros is full of—smiles.

I nodded. "We might go this weekend."

Athena flipped her long, straight, light brown hair. "My cousin had a cat and once it pooped in her bed. She forgot to make her bed one day, and that night, when she climbed into bed, she got cat poop all over her. Gross. Plus they caught the cat eating the Thanksgiving turkey that they'd left on the table after dinner and had to throw it away. Also gross. And then they found it in the crib with her baby brother and her dad decided it had to go."

"I'm still getting a cat, Athena."

"Just saying. Pets are a lot of work." Another thing Athena is full of—advice.

"Some pets," I corrected her.

"They should have a place where you could rent a pet for maybe a week, and if you like it you can keep it, but if you don't you can bring it back." Sometimes Athena talks too much and this was definitely one of those times. "Plus cats are boring, don't you think?" she added.

"Yep, usually they're quiet." I stopped walking and put my finger to my mouth as if to say shhh.

Athena got the hint and changed the subject. "We might go to Italy for a week. My grandma wants me to see Rome."

"Yay! Athena goes to Rome. I'll be thinking about that while I'm in my room with my boring cat and stinky litter box all summer."

Athena made a sad face. "Sorry . . . Wish you could come, too, V."

Because I knew she meant it, I smiled. But in my mind, I daydreamed that I was going with her. Then, I silently wished I had grandparents who lived far away and wanted me to come for a long visit. All I have are Gam and Poppy, who live right around the corner.

My thoughts must have shown on my face, because Athena blurted, "Would you stop the sad looks? I'll keep in touch. Plus, it's not like you're friendless . . . you still have Yaz," she reminded me.

Yaz, short for Yazmine, is my kinda-sorta-good friend, a girl who doesn't go to school with us but who I know from the ice skating rink. For Yaz Kilroy, ice skating is everything.

"But she hardly ever does regular stuff like us, only skating," I said.

Athena agreed, "Yeah, I know."

A little silence followed.

"You're flying all the way by yourself, huh?"

Athena put out her hand and shook it nervously. "For the first time."

In minutes, we reached her house, which is right down the street from mine.

"You gotta send me a gazillion postcards like you said. And if you meet a cute boy, promise not to forget about me like Daisy." Since my sister, Daisy, got her new boy-friend, Wyatt, it seemed like she barely had time for me anymore. Another reason I could safely predict this was going to be a summer of boring nothing.

"I won't," Athena promised, and we stared at each other for what seemed like a long time until tears got in our eyes.

Finally, Athena gave me a big bright grin and hugged me tight.

I smiled what Poppy calls a counterfeit smile, day-dreamed once more that I was going with her, said good-bye, and headed home.

If boredom was like macaroni without cheese, what I felt right then was worse. Lemonade without sugar, soda without the fizz. Pitiful.

3

SOMETIMES I WISH

With Athena gone, I was walking home alone from my last day of elementary school when just like that, dark gray clouds that mean it's going to rain for certain gathered and turned the almost-summer air cold. I didn't have my umbrella and wasn't even wearing a hoodie. Lucky Violet.

I needed to run fast and that's exactly what I was about to do when I heard what sounded like crying, so I stopped and listened. There it was again—not a cry, a cat's meow. I followed the mews until I found it curled up under a tree in front of a house, a kitten with spotted fur, almost like a leopard. I kneeled down and gently stroked its little head, but the kitten's eyes were crusted shut and wouldn't open. I dug through my backpack, found a napkin, dampened it with water from my water bottle, and carefully wiped away the crust. Before long, it opened its eyes, and I smiled because the kitten's eyes were hazel . . . the same green-blue-brown color eyes as my mom's and Daisy's.

"How did you get here?" I asked as I picked it up and cradled it like a baby. I had been wishing for a cat for months. Maybe we wouldn't have to get one from the shelter after all. Was it possible that one of my wishes was finally coming true? I smiled inside and out.

The kitten opened its mouth wide and let out a really loud "Meow!"

"You sure are a loud mouth."

Again, "Meow!" This time louder and longer.

"A really loud mouth," I proclaimed.

The sound of a door opening made me turn toward the house I was standing in front of. An old lady peeked out. "What you got there, Curly?" she asked.

My hair is long and—guess what—curly. No, not just curly—corkscrew curly. And if one more person calls me Curly, I'm going to scream.

"A kitten," I replied.

"That so?" the woman said as she came outside and hobbled with a cane down her walkway toward me. Her short hair was snow white and her skin so wrinkly, it looked like someone had ironed creases in it.

Please don't let the kitten belong to her.

She stared at the kitten for a while, then stroked its spotted fur. "Where do you suppose it came from?"

I sighed. "It's not yours?"

"No, not mine." She grinned at the kitten, then at me. "Looks hungry, though. Maybe needs some milk." She began walking back to her door. "C'mon, Curly."

"My name's Violet, not Curly," I informed her as I grabbed my backpack and trailed her to the door.

"Well, c'mon, Vi," she said.

"It's not Vi, either, just Violet, or call me V. That's what most people call me."

"I like Violet better," the old lady commented as she reached to open the screen door.

"That's how it is these days, kind of. I mean, lots of people call other people by the first initial of their name. Like, instead of calling my sister Daisy, I call her D."

"Violet and Daisy? Your parents must have a penchant for flowers."

Penchant? I'd have to add that to my book of words I'd never heard before. "What's a penchant?"

"Means 'a strong liking for something.'" She paused. "But violet's also a color . . . reddish blue."

"It's also the name for a small butterfly that belongs to the family Lycaenidae." I love telling people that because it usually makes them think I'm incredibly smart. I could tell by the look in her eyes that this lady was instantly added to my list of *people who think Violet Diamond is incredibly smart.*

"Really? I didn't know that. So you're an entomologist."

"A person who studies insects? Nope . . . I seriously hate bugs. Seriously."

Her face crinkled into a smile. "Me too," she agreed as she motioned me inside. "Wipe your feet."

The old lady seemed pretty normal, but no way was I going inside a stranger's house. "I'll wait here," I told her.

"Okay, Violet . . . or V."

"What's your name?" I asked.

"Georgina," she replied.

"So, I might just call you G. Get it?"

She grinned and her eyes, which were as blue as Gam's, sparkled. "Got it," she replied, stepping inside the house.

Before long, she came back with a small bowl of milk, but her hands were pretty shaky and some of it spilled as she set it down. "Getting old."

I put the kitten down and nudged it close to the bowl. Quickly, it lapped the milk, and when it seemed like it was full, the spotted kitty sat back and let out another extremely loud meow.

"Loud mouth," I said.

"So you could name it LM for Loud Mouth," G suggested.

I hadn't even thought about a name. "LM? It's not

really a cat name," I said, then asked, "So you think I should keep it? I mean, do you think it belongs to someone around here?"

"So many strays around here, it's a crime. Save me from having to call Animal Control one more time. Yes, V, I definitely think you should keep it, if it's okay with your parents."

"It's just my mom."

"Oh," G said with a sad voice, the way some grown-ups do when I tell them that "it's just my mom."

When G opened her mouth to talk again, I figured *here come the questions. Not today,* I thought. May as well tell her. "My dad is dead." G's eyes looked the way my insides suddenly felt, sad. "But I have a really nice grandpa," I added. The old lady's eyes turned happy. That should be the end of that, I hoped.

It was, because G sighed, "That's nice."

Right then thunder clapped. Before long, it was going to pour.

Georgina gazed up. "You hurry home now, V," she ordered.

I scooped up the kitten and was busy thanking G for the milk when humungous drops of rain began polka-dotting the street, sidewalk, and walkway. It was only three blocks to my house, but still, no matter how fast I ran, I was bound to get soaked.

Just as I prepared to bolt, Georgina asked, "Don't you have an umbrella?"

I shook my head. "No."

"Wait here. I have extras."

Around here, most people have more than one umbrella. My grandpa claims that in our town, Moon Lake, Washington, umbrellas are big business. Moon Lake is not too far from Seattle. In Moon Lake, it rains—a lot.

While G was inside, I carefully placed the kitten in my backpack. "We'll be home soon," I said. Another very loud meow.

"Thank you," I told the lady when she handed me the umbrella. "I'll bring it back tomorrow . . . I promise."

"Keep it. I have a grand collection."

I thanked her again, opened the umbrella, clutched the backpack to my chest with one arm, and took off.

4

INTRODUCING
VIOLET DIAMOND'S KITTEN

The rain hit the street hard—thousands of bouncing liquid balls. And because I mostly used the umbrella to keep the backpack dry, by the time I made it home, I was sopping wet. My soaked feet were cold and my hand trembled as I turned the key in the lock. Luckily the house was toasty warm. I like toasty warm.

The house was quiet. I also like quiet. "Anybody home?" I asked.

"Up here!" my grandma called out. "Working on the computer." My grandma works from our house during the day. "There are some snacks in the fridge!"

I laid the backpack on the floor and carefully lifted out the kitten. Thankfully, it was dry. "You okay?" I asked,

14

and kissed its tiny head. "I love you," I told it. "Do you love me, too?"

When it responded with a loud mew, I decided that meant yes. I gazed into its hazel eyes and stroked its furry head. I was definitely in love. "I'll take good care of you," I promised the kitten.

Quickly, I climbed the steps and sped to Gam's office. "I found a cat," I said, and proudly presented the loud-mouthed kitten.

As usual, Gam was sitting at her desk, her reading glasses at the tip of her nose, her grayish blond hair hanging in her face. She glanced up, smiled, and stared at the kitty. "Cute," she said. She started to get up from her desk, but when her business phone rang, she sat back down. "Get out of those wet things, V . . . Hello?"

"I will," I told her, and headed back downstairs. My body shivered and I knew I should change into dry clothes, but the in-love part of me dashed to the kitchen, where I grabbed a bowl, poured in some milk, and scooted the kitten toward it. Patiently, I waited for it to do something, but it just stood still.

"Meow!" I supposed it wanted cat food.

"You have to understand . . . I never, ever get things I wish for. Plus I just wished for you two days ago. So I don't have any cat food or a litter box or any of that stuff."

I was thinking *what am I doing, talking to it like it*

understands English, when the kitchen door swung open and Daisy burst inside, noisy and swirling, like a mini tornado. Daisy is tall and extremely pretty and, just like the flower she gets her name from, sunny and happy.

"It was *so* not supposed to rain today, was it?" she asked.

"Nope . . . but it did," I replied.

Her long, wet blond hair, plastered to her head, looked dark, and her eyes were black underneath like a raccoon from runny mascara. She's a high school junior and supposed to be saving for college, but every cent she makes from her part-time job is spent on makeup and clothes.

Daisy tripped over the bowl of milk, which spilled, and fell hard—right on her butt. Another thing about D is she's one of the clumsiest people in the universe. Not even her yoga classes have helped.

"Ce que le diable!" Daisy said in French, then immediately translated into English the way she has a habit of doing. "What the heck!" Daisy is into all things French. She's even considering going to the Sorbonne after graduation. Even her boyfriend is part French.

But even wet and clumsy, Daisy was still what her boyfriend, Wyatt, called her the other day—breathtaking—which I found out means "astonishingly beautiful."

Will I ever be breathtaking?

I reached out my hand and helped her up off the floor. "You okay, D?" I asked.

Her eyes landed on the bowl of milk. "Explain, please."

I grinned and pointed at the kitten, which had run to a corner of the room. "I got a wish, finally."

"*Le chat mignon* . . . cute cat, V!" She picked up the kitten, which was only a little bigger than the palm of her hand, and kissed its head. "What's its name?"

"I don't know. It's a stray. I found it on the way home from school."

My sister wrapped a wet arm around me and we huddled together, staring at the small spotted cat. "I got a wish, finally," I repeated.

Daisy and I may not look alike, but we are the same in some ways and different in others. Both of our fathers were medical doctors, but her father died of cancer when she was two years old and my father died in a car wreck two months before I was born, so neither of us has a dad. But my father adopted Daisy when he and my mom got married, so at least we have the same last name. We also both like traveling. One way we're not the same is I like quiet—she likes loud. But the main difference is Daisy's father was white and my father was African American. Mom, who calls her family a European conglomeration, has peachy skin and naturally blond hair, just like Daisy. So, my sister, Daisy, is white, but I am brown haired, brown eyed, brown skinned, biracial.

In some bigger cities, like Seattle, there are lots of biracial kids. But Moon Lake is mostly white. And there are only two other biracial kids in my school, a girl and her younger brother whose dad is black and mom is white. They look just alike—light skinned with green eyes and light brown hair. Lucky for them, they have each other. As for me, I sometimes feel like a single fallen brown leaf atop a blanket of fresh snow. Alone.

When some people meet my mom and me for the first time, they get that funny question-mark look in their eyes. Then their inner lightbulb goes on and I can tell that they've figured out that I'm biracial. Even when I'm with my mom's parents, Poppy and Gam, people seem to understand. But for some reason, when Daisy's along and introduced as my sister, it causes confusion. Poppy *usually always* smiles at the person and gives them the peace sign, but Mom or Gam *usually always* takes my hand, as if to say I belong to them, which I do. And even though I know they love me, at moments when people stare like that, I still wish I could vanish.

Stop thinking about things you can't change, Violet.

The house was getting extremely toasty warm again and the kitty yawned.

"Boy or girl cat?" D asked.

I shrugged. "I dunno."

"Did you tell Mom yet?"

"I was going to surprise her," I said, but the truth was I hadn't even thought about it.

"Well, make sure it doesn't have fleas or any animal diseases," she said as she headed to her room. "And you should take off those wet clothes and clean up that milk," she commanded. Like most older sisters, Daisy is the boss.

"After I do, will you take me to the pet store? I have my own money," I asked.

"It's raining," she replied.

"So?"

She had that look on her face that said she really didn't want to, but for some reason, maybe because I'd finally gotten a wish, she said, "Okay, in a little while."

I cleaned up the mess and was heading to my cave with the kitten when the back door opened again. This time it was Poppy, my grandpa.

Poppy and Gam live close by and they're at our house or we're at theirs so much, it's sort of like we all live together. Either Gam or Poppy are always here when I get home from school because Mom has funny hours at the hospital where she works in the NICU—Neonatal Intensive Care Unit—as a doctor who takes care of teeny-tiny just-born babies.

Poppy is taller than six feet with skin that's starting to get wrinkly, especially around his eyes when he smiles. He wears his gray hair long and sometimes in a ponytail.

"Hi, Poppy."

Poppy kissed me on the forehead and asked, "How's my girl?"

I was about to tell him about the cat when he started fussing about his umbrella. He couldn't get it to close. "I swear they make umbrellas to break! They could make umbrellas to last a lifetime if they wanted! And this idiotic rain interrupted my golf game!"

Patiently, I waited for him to notice the kitten I was holding.

Finally, he did. "Whose cat?"

"Mine. Mom said I could have one this morning. And guess what—today I found one."

"Serendipity," Poppy proclaimed as he patted the kitten's head.

Another new word to add to my book. That was two in just one day. But before I could ask what it meant, Poppy gave me the answer. "Means 'getting what you want by what seems like chance' . . . What's its name?"

"I didn't give it one yet. It's a stray. Don't know if it's a boy or girl. I don't have any food or a bed for it or anything. But Daisy promised to take me to the pet store in a little while."

Poppy touched my shoulder. My clothes were still wet. He didn't have to say a word. The look he gave me told me I needed to get out of wet clothes and into dry ones in a hurry. "I know," I said. "Put on dry clothes."

I gave him a peck on the cheek and handed him the kitten. "Thanks," I told him, and rushed to my room.

On my way, I passed D's door and knocked twice. "I'll be ready in a minute."

"Yeah, yeah!" she yelled.

In my cave, I changed my clothes fast, grabbed my word book, and wrote down *penchant* and *serendipity.* The definitions would have to wait.

"Serendipity," I said out loud, and smiled.

I hope I get some more of it.

5

DAISY'S LI'L SIS

At the pet store, the lady told us it was a girl cat and I decided on the name Hazel because of her eyes.

"It's a cute name," Daisy agreed.

Unfortunately, because I bought a cartload of stuff, I was a few dollars short at the checkout counter.

"You should put back the rhinestone collar," Daisy said.

"Please," I begged, grinning. "After all, I am your favorite sister."

"*Vous êtes ma seule soeur,*" Daisy replied as she dug out the extra money I needed and handed it to the cashier.

"In English, please," I replied.

"You're my only sister," Daisy translated.

"She's your sister?" the woman asked Daisy.

"Obviously," Daisy replied.

The woman glanced from me to Daisy and then back

at me, doing that thing I hate—like she was trying to figure out the answer to a riddle.

Inside, I felt like a miniature volcano that needed to erupt.

You're an imbecile, an ignoramus, a moron!

Leave the stuff on the counter.

Grab Daisy's hand and leave.

But I didn't cause a scene in the store. Instead, like I do when I'm really mad at someone, I glared at the lady, took a deep breath, breathed out through my nose, and imagined fire shooting out like a dragon.

Outside, Daisy took the change the cashier had given her and dropped it in my hand. "You owe me."

I threw the bag of stuff in the car, slammed the door, cuddled Hazel, and frowned.

"Please take that poor-Violet-feeling-sorry-for-herself look off your face," Daisy told me.

"What?"

"The look you always get when someone looks at us weird or asks a ridiculous question like that cashier did."

So, Daisy does notice . . .

"I don't like it when that happens . . . and it makes me mad," I said.

"Welcome to Earth. Some people are stupid. She's one of them. You have to get over it."

I erupted on Daisy. "Get over it? You don't understand! You're not me!"

"And you're not me!" she snapped back.

"You're right! I'm not the breathtaking queen of the world!"

Everything went hush and time froze.

But when we pulled into the driveway, Daisy sighed, said, "Sorry, V," and reached for my hand.

I jerked away. "Too late," I grumbled. "Way too late," I whispered, and was climbing out of the car when Daisy tugged on my jacket and sat me back down.

Softly, she said, "For the record, I don't like it when people do that, either, but that's their problem. This is not about them, it's about us. Try not to let it upset you. You're my li'l sis and I love you, and no brainless zombie creature can change that. Chill."

Li'l sis. I like it when she calls me that. I took a very deep breath and sighed. "Love you, too," I told her.

Later that night, when Mom came into my room, I put aside the book I was reading and we both admired Hazel for a very long time, but I was still upset about the lady in the pet store and it must have shown. Mom cupped my face in her hand and gazed into my eyes. Like the warm sun, so much love shone from her. "Is everything okay, Violet?"

Mom is good at lots of things, especially worrying about me.

Part of me wanted to tell her about some of the stuff

I felt inside—that sometimes I had a strange loneliness and that I got tired of idiotic questions and how I hated being the only black kid in class this past year and how I wished there were more African American people in Moon Lake so I wouldn't always stand out so much and how I already missed Athena—but the other part of me decided to keep quiet. *After all,* I thought as I glanced around my pretty purple room with the four-poster bed, flat-screen TV, and computer, *we live in a very nice house and I have more cool stuff than any girl could want.*

"Yes," I replied, "everything is okay."

"Okay, but if you need to talk—"

I interrupted, "I know . . . you have ears." It's one of her sayings.

She kissed the top of my head and was about to leave when I asked her, "Where do dreams come from?"

"Sometimes a secret wish or the inner mind's way of working out something from the subconscious," she replied.

"Deeper than our real thoughts?"

"Yes. Are you having bad dreams, V?" Mom asked.

"No, but I had a very cool one." The look she gave me told me she wanted me to keep on talking, so I did. "We were on vacation . . . me, you, Daisy . . ." I hesitated. "And my dad. In the dream, he hugged me. We were a real family. So I suppose my inner mind knows my wishes."

"A real family?" she asked.

"With a dad and a mom. Like Yaz and Athena have."

"Real families come in many shapes, Violet, you know that."

"I know. I just wish he didn't die."

Mom's face turned sad. "I wish that, too, Violet."

"But it wasn't a sad dream. It was the best dream I ever had. I even wrote it down in my word and wish journal under a new section."

"It's important for you to understand that some wishes can't come true, Violet, no matter what," she told me.

"I know."

"And others can. Like Hazel," she said as she stroked the kitten. "And sometimes, a wish combined with hard work can make it a reality. Like when I was a girl, I wished I could be a doctor, but then I worked hard to make that wish come true. You understand?"

"I really do."

"I'm glad. Love you. Good night," she said. But before she closed my door, she added, "I have the two best daughters in the world . . . wouldn't change either of you for anything. Don't stay up too late."

"I won't," I promised.

I showered, climbed into bed, and snuggled Hazel. "I finally got a wish," I said to the sky.

6

A BEGINNING

The day I found Hazel was the day I began to believe that some wishes can come true.

Now, I still make wishes, but only for things that I figure are possible, because I don't ever want to go back to thinking that wishing is a waste of time. But like Mom says, sometimes you have to work to make your wishes come true.

Like wishing I could do a perfect Axel at the ice skating rink, and I practiced over and over again until finally one day I did.

"Now try a double," my friend Yaz encouraged me.

Yaz has light brown skin, braided hair, and six freckles on each cheek. I know because I counted them. Yaz is constantly giving me skin and hair care advice. Stuff my mom spent a lot of online time trying to help me with, but until I told her about Yaz's recommendations, I hadn't been successful. Now, thanks to Yaz, instead of tangles and frizz, my curls are soft and bouncy and my skin is never ashy.

We really don't look alike, but because we're both black, when people see us together, they assume we're sisters. But by now, just like no one thinking Daisy is my sister, I'm used to most people thinking Yaz is. And sometimes when I'm with her and her mom, dad, brother, and sister, people think I belong to them. I would never tell anyone, but I have to admit, sometimes that feels nice.

Yaz plans to be the first African American female to get an ice skating gold medal at the Olympics, and ice skating is her world. For me, ice skating is fun—a small piece of my pie-of-life. Plus, I like to be warm and cozy a little too much to hang out at the rink every day.

"I can't do a double."

"Watch me, it's easy," she said.

My eyes followed Yaz as she glided on the ice, vaulted over the toe pick of her left skate, and stepped up into the jump with her right leg. Once Yaz starts, she's unstoppable. She uncrossed her legs on the perfect landing, grinned, and skated toward me.

"You can do it, V, just try once."

"I'm proud of the single Axel," I told her. Plus, falling on the ice hurts and I wasn't in the mood.

"Just try," she repeated.

"No can do!" I replied, and floated off to do something I am extremely good at instead, figure eights.

"Boring!" Yaz called out.

There's more to life than ice skating, I thought, and wished again that Athena was around. When Athena comes to the rink with us, it's so much better. Even Yaz relaxes and has more fun—the three of us just having a good time gliding around and around on the ice, making a few spins, racing to see who's the fastest, joking, laughing, getting pizza at the snack bar. Athena + anything *usually always* = better fun.

Yaz sped toward me on the ice and skidded to a stop. "You can do a double Axel. I just know it. At least try. Don't be a quitter, Violet," she badgered. It was worse than being nagged at home to help with the dishes or clean my room.

I made a silent wish. *Please send Athena back. Please.*

7

ANOTHER WISH COMES TRUE

Three days of the first week of summer vacation had been spent at the rink, taking a class. I was never going to win any awards, but like Mom and Yaz finally convinced me, there is always room for improvement. The other days I helped Gam with her vegetable garden, and one day a week was set aside to spend with Poppy learning golf, which is much harder than it looks. Even my favorite thing, putting, takes what Poppy calls great skill.

The following Saturday morning, the doorbell rang. Mom had already left for the hospital, Gam and Poppy were sleeping in late in the spare bedroom where they stay on the nights Mom is on call, and Daisy was in the shower. I put my eye to the peephole and couldn't believe my eyes.

Athena was back!

I screamed and threw open the door at the same time. "You're back!"

We hugged and jumped up and down. "This wishing stuff is really working," I told her.

"Wishing stuff?" Athena asked.

"I wished that you would come back," I explained. "And you did."

"Wishing had nothing to do with it, V," Athena replied, and went on to tell me that she'd come back early because her mother had given birth to her baby brother more than a month ahead of time and her grandma wanted to be with her mom.

Because of the kind of doctor my mom is, a worry signal went off inside me. I didn't want to start jumping for joy about Athena being back if there was a problem with her new brother. "Is the baby okay?" I asked.

"Healthy and cute," Athena said.

"What's his name?" I asked.

"Diogenes, after some Greek philosopher." Athena's parents are into ancient Greek stuff. "But everyone is calling him Dio. I wanted to name him a normal name like Evan or Blake."

"But Dio sounds kinda cool," I told her.

"Yeah, if you're in Greece."

"You're really back! This is too awesome!" I yelled. And as I dragged her to my cave, I informed her, "I have a new family member, too." I scooped up my kitten. "Introducing Hazel. Do you like the name?"

"I do. Plus she's so adorable," Athena gushed. "I want a kitty."

"Just wish for one, like I did," I told her. "I wish for stuff every night before I go to sleep."

"You mean pray, right?"

"To God?" I asked.

"Of course, genius, who else?"

Unlike my family, Athena's goes to church every Sunday and prays at mealtime. At my house, Mom mentions God sometimes and Daisy told me that when she was little, my mom and dad used to take her to church every Sunday. But after my dad died, Mom stopped going.

Athena changed the subject. "Did you notice my hair is lighter?" She flipped her hair with her hand.

It was, but only a few smidgens. I like the word *smidgen*. "It's pretty."

"My cousin in Athens did it for me. She put color on it to make it look sun-kissed. Does it look sun-kissed?"

I nodded.

Maybe if my hair were lighter, people would stop asking stupid questions. Maybe I'd look a little like Daisy and Mom. Maybe I'd be breathtaking.

"Could you color mine—make it sun-kissed?"

Athena stood behind me and fingered my curls.

"Okay," she agreed. "It'll look awesome. Trust me."

. . .

The drugstore had so many kinds of hair dye, it was almost impossible to choose. I started getting a little nervous and wished Yaz were here to help. Finally, we decided on a color.

"This for your mother?" the checkout lady asked us.

Athena lied, "Yes," and handed her the money.

When we got back to my house, I made a silent wish that Poppy was off doing his favorite thing, playing golf, but he was doing his second-favorite thing, cooking. "Where've you been, V?"

I clutched the bag with the hair color tightly. "At the drugstore . . . Gam said I could go."

Poppy eyed the bag. "Whatcha got?"

Usually it takes me a while to dream up a lie, but this one just came right out. "Kitty stuff."

"Oh," he said, and went back to cooking. "Have a seat, little ladies. You're just in time for lunch. I made my famous shrimp quesadillas."

It smelled so good, we had to say yes. Hair coloring would have to wait.

When we were done, we helped with the dishes and were heading to my room when Poppy called out. He held up the bag from the drugstore. "Hey, V. You forgot your *kitty* stuff." Something in the way he said it made me think he didn't buy the lie.

And he was opening it up to peek inside when I took it from his hand. "Thanks, Poppy," I said, smiling sweetly.

Athena laughed.

We cuddled Hazel and read the directions.

"We need something to mix the dye in," Athena said.

That meant venturing back into the kitchen. I tiptoed down the hall. Lucky for me, Poppy was now in the family room, practicing on his indoor putting green and watching golf on TV.

I retrieved a bowl and small wooden spoon from the kitchen.

"It says if your hair is dark, you have to leave it on a little longer."

"Okay."

Athena parted my hair into four sections and said, "You sure have a lot of hair."

"For real, huh?"

"And it's so pretty and curly."

"Duh."

"Maybe I should call you Curly," Athena joked.

"Not."

Before long, my hair was covered with dye. We put on the plastic cap, and while we waited we played video games and yakked.

"Was Greece really pretty?" I asked.

"As pretty as Hawaii," Athena claimed. "But my grandparents' house is way up on the side of a hill, so there were a gazillion steps."

"What did you do there?"

"We walked around some ancient ruins," she answered.

"And what else?"

"I met a very awesome boy."

"For real?" This was getting interesting.

"But he's my first cousin."

"Oh," I replied disappointedly.

"But I met another cute boy, too."

"And?"

Athena cackled. "Also my first cousin."

"You are so lying," I told her.

"Am not," Athena declared.

I doubled over and belly laughed.

We looked at photos she had taken in Greece on the computer, including those of her two very cute boy cousins, and made a pinkie-finger pact to beg her parents and my mom to let me go with her next time she went.

After a while, I asked Athena, "It seems like it's been a long time, doesn't it?"

Athena glanced at her watch. "Oh no," she blurted, yanked my arm, and led me to the sink. She rinsed out the dye, washed my hair, and said, "Hmm . . ."

"That doesn't sound good," I told her.

"It's . . . different than I thought it would be."

I sprang up and stared at myself in the mirror. "No! My hair! What happened to just sun-kissed?"

"Maybe we left it on too long," Athena said nervously, "but I kinda like it. It's sort of copper colored."

"I don't want copper hair!" I told Athena.

Athena tried hard to calm me down. "After we blow it dry and flat iron it, it should look cool."

My mom's going to murder me!

A knock on my bedroom door. "Violet?" It was Gam. Gam didn't believe in closed doors unless you were a teenager. She turned the knob and cracked the door. "Violet?" she repeated.

In a flash, I shut the door to my bathroom, quickly wrapped a towel turban style around my head, and frantically hid the hair stuff in the vanity. "We're in the bathroom. Athena is doing my hair," I hollered out.

"What's that smell?" Gam asked as she gently pushed the bathroom door open. "Hi, Athena," Gam added, sniffing the room.

"It's a new hair product . . . from Greece," Athena said.

"Or maybe the kitty litter," I added.

Gam glanced at Hazel, who was resting comfortably on the bed, and sniffed again. "Maybe that's it."

"Athena is going to flat iron it straight." I scooted past Gam and headed to Daisy's room for the blow dryer and flat iron.

Gam protested, "But your curls are beautiful. I always wished I had curly hair."

Athena chimed in again, "My mom claims we always want what we don't have."

"Maybe she's right, but open the window for some fresh air," Gam said as she left.

Athena turned me away from the mirror while she blew my hair dry and flat ironed it pin straight. "Wow, I never noticed it before . . . you really look like Daisy," Athena proclaimed.

Finally, someone noticed the family resemblance! About that, I felt happy. I only hoped my hair wasn't ruined.

Athena painted my lips with her pink lip gloss and turned me around to the mirror.

Now that my hair was dry, it was orange. I felt like crying.

And that's when my mom, Justine Diamond, M.D., knocked on my door. "I got off early, V. Want to go to the movies?"

I'm dead.

I hid in the closet.

"Hi, Justine," Athena said.

"Oh! Hi, Athena. I thought you were in Greece."

"No, I came back early because my mom had the baby and his name is Dio and he's really cute and plus my grandma is here, too, so you should come over and see them when you get a chance."

"I'll do that," Mom told her. "Where's Violet?"

"In the closet."

I sank to the floor, closed my eyes tightly, and silently wished that this wasn't happening. But when I opened my eyes and looked at a section of my hair, which was still orange, I knew this wish had not been granted.

8

NOT EXACTLY
WHAT I WAS EXPECTING

Silence as the closet door opened wide.

Mom stared at me like I was a creature from another galaxy.

"Hi," I whispered.

Athena bounced up off the bed. "I should be going."

"Yes, you should be going, Athena," Mom told her.

Athena left and Mom closed the door behind her. Her face looked like she'd been stung by a bee. "What? Why?" she asked.

"I wasn't expecting it to be this color."

"What were you expecting?"

I shrugged my shoulders. "I dunno . . . for it to be lighter. I just wanted to look like you and Daisy."

Mom plopped on the bed. "You do look like me and Daisy."

"Not to me I don't." I paused for a few seconds and added, "And I wanted to be beautiful."

Mom stood up, came over to the closet, and pulled me up. She put her arms around me and hugged me. "You are beautiful, V."

"It's just sometimes I wish we all looked the same, Mom."

Mom held my face in her hands. "There are two beautiful sides to you, the black side and the white side."

"But all I know is the white side."

Her face got that stung-by-a-bee look again.

Mom glanced over at my photo wall, stared at the big photo of my father, and started to cry. "Your father, Warren, was the dearest man I ever knew. Sometimes when I look at you, I can see him, especially when you smile. You were his gift to me . . . a part of him that lives on. I wish you had known him."

So do I.

I expected Daisy to laugh when she saw me, but all she did was inspect my hair and ask, "What were you thinking? You had such great hair and you probably ruined it."

"Athena said it would look . . . sun-kissed."

Daisy rolled her eyes. "But what did your inner voice tell you?"

"My inner voice? What's that?"

"That thing inside that warns you," she replied.

"Oh, that."

Daisy placed her hand on her hip. "Well?"

"It said . . . maybe this is a bad idea. But I didn't listen and went ahead anyway."

"And paid the price," Daisy said.

"Yep."

Daisy ran her fingers through my damaged hair again. "Huge mistake. Listen to your inner voice, li'l sis, *promets*?"

"Huh?"

"Promise?" Daisy said.

"Promise," I replied.

Gam frantically called her beauty salon. They were booked solid for the rest of the day, and tomorrow was Sunday. Nine a.m. Monday was the best they could do.

"Kitty stuff, huh?" Poppy asked with a wink.

Why did I suddenly feel like I was the only one in the family who had ever made a mistake?

I wish they would all disappear.

9

THE UNIVERSE OF VIOLET DIAMOND TAKES A SWERVE

Against the rules, I locked myself up in my room and barricaded the door with my nightstand. I put my earphones in, turned on my iPod, and held Hazel close to my heart. The day passed.

"Pizza's here!" Poppy knocked and yelled. It was almost dark out.

"Not hungry!"

A few minutes later, another knock.

"Go away! I'm not coming out of my room!"

This time it was Mom. "Pepperoni. Get it while it's hot . . . some juice, too. I'll leave it by the door," she said.

"I hate cold pizza," I told Hazel as I grabbed the pizza

and juice bottle. And much later, when I figured everyone was asleep, I headed to the kitchen to feed my kitty.
But on the way back to my room, I heard voices. Mom
and Gam were talking in Mom's bedroom. I heard my
name, so I stood there and eavesdropped.

"Haven't I always taught Violet about African American history?"

"Don't take this so personally, Justine. This is normal
kid stuff. You're making it a race issue."

As if Mom hadn't heard her, she asked more questions. "Haven't I encouraged her to be friends with Yaz
and her family? And taken her to the Dance Theatre of
Harlem and Alvin Ailey? And don't we spend almost
every Thanksgiving with the Nevilles?"

Mrs. Neville was Mom's good friend from work who's
a speech therapist—and black.

"Stop it, Justine."

"It's not enough, is it? I should be doing more. Maybe
we should move back to Seattle so she's not so isolated.
It's my fault. She only knows the white side. That's what
she told me," Mom said tearfully.

"It's true, Justine. But it's not your fault."

"I'm calling *her* again."

Who was *her*? I wondered.

"You sure that's wise? She never returns your phone
messages or answers your cards or letters."

"She's Warren's mother. I want Violet to know her."

"She knows where to find you. All this nonsense because her son married a white woman."

"There's more to it than that and you know it," Mom said.

"Justine! The accident was not your fault."

"Yes, it was," Mom sobbed.

"Hush," Gam whispered.

Silence followed.

Quieter than a mouse, I tiptoed down the hall to my room, closed the door, and plopped on the bed. The accident was her fault? I'd never heard anyone say that before. What had happened? Hazel nuzzled my pant leg, so I picked her up. "What else don't I know?" I asked out loud.

The accident was her fault? The question repeated over and over in my head. I got up and stared at my father's photograph on my photo wall.

Then my eyes shifted to our family reunion pictures from past summers. The white faces of Mom's family, my aunts/uncles/cousins, stared back at me. It's always easy to pick me out, the only brown person. Just like in my class pictures.

Next, I looked at the photograph of my dad's mother and father that hangs right next to his. I knew my father's dad had died while my dad was in medical school. He and my father almost looked like twins. Finally, I examined the *her* Mom and Gam must have been talking about, my father's mother—my other grandmother, Roxanne Diamond.

My middle name is Roxanne, after her, but I've never met her or even talked to her on the phone. And when I was little, I used to wonder about why I never got to see her. Whenever I asked, I got answers from Mom like "she travels a lot" or "she's living in Europe." So, after a while, I just stopped asking. The way no one ever mentioned her name, it was as if Roxanne Diamond was kind of dead.

Even if she is mad at my mom, doesn't Roxanne Diamond at least care about me?

Gloomy clouds got in my mind again and I felt sorry for myself. I had every right to, didn't I?

Daisy's grandparents on her father's side are always sending her cards and presents and stuff, and almost every Christmas either Daisy goes to Connecticut for two weeks or they come to Washington to spend time with her. Plus, Athena spends every other summer in Greece with her grandparents. That's what grandparents are supposed to do, right?

I turned on my computer, and as I'd done a few times before, but not lately, I searched for the name *Roxanne Diamond*.

Thousands of results popped up. Quickly, I went to her website. She had new stuff on her pages, mostly photographs. A photo of her at a gallery stared back at me. She looked a lot older than the picture that's on my wall, but it was definitely *her*. My grandmother, Roxanne Kamaria Diamond, the famous artist. Recently, it said, she'd moved back to California.

As I scrolled down her website, I came to some photographs of her when she was a girl and stopped. I gasped. One of the photos looked a lot like me. I went to the mirror and stared at my reflection.

Questions I wanted answers to were on my mind. Why was Roxanne Diamond acting like I didn't exist? Why was the accident my mom's fault? And what other secrets were being kept from me?

10

TRUTH AND TEARS

Ever since I can remember, Sunday hikes with Mom are one of those *usually always* things. It used to be me, Mom, and Daisy time, but between Daisy's job and Wyatt, the boyfriend, she hardly ever comes with us anymore. Today Daisy had to work, so Mom and I packed a lunch and were off to the lake. Because I had so many questions, I was glad we were going to be alone.

I tied a bandanna around my head and put on a baseball hat to keep people from gawking at my orange curls. Tomorrow at nine, my hair would be back to normal, I hoped. With skin so brown, I felt like I looked totally bizarre. I didn't like it—at all.

We hiked for a while, until we got to this huge boulder where we decided to rest. In silence, we watched the blue water ripple on the lake. Mom and I both like quiet. But today I needed some answers.

I took an extremely deep breath before I said these words because I was worried about upsetting my mom. I hate it when she gets that look like she's been stung by an insect. On the other hand, there were things I had to know. I exhaled. "She's an artist."

"Who?"

"My dad's mom, Roxanne Diamond."

As expected, the stung-by-a-bee look covered her face. "How did you find that out?"

"On the Internet."

"Of course."

"Is she from Africa?" I asked.

"No . . . why would you think that?"

"Because in her pictures she's *usually always* dressed in African clothes and her paintings are mostly of African people."

"She was born in New York City, V, but she's always been very Afrocentric."

A cool new word. "Afrocentric?"

"A person who's very interested in the history and culture of Africa and black people. She used to teach African art history, and while she was in college, she didn't call herself Roxanne; she went by an African name."

"Kamaria?"

"I think so. How did you know that?"

"It's online, too. It means 'like the moon.' It's her middle name."

Mom cracked a grin and squeezed my head to her shoulder. "You've done good research."

"Yep . . . her website says she lives in Los Angeles now."

"Really? She travels a lot, and she lived in Paris and Berlin and Nairobi for years, but she's always had a house in Los Angeles." Mom sighed. "She's just different. Artists sometimes are. She's bohemian."

"Bohemian? Where's that country?"

"It just means she lives an unconventional life."

Bohemian? Unconventional? Two more new words. Well, I suppose if they mean the same thing, it's really only one new word. "English, please?"

"She doesn't live an ordinary life."

"Oh . . . you mean not boring?"

"Yes, not boring."

"She's pretty, huh?"

"Yes, she is."

"Did she ever see me . . . ever? Like when I was a baby?"

"She's never seen you in person, but every year I send her pictures of you," Mom replied, then got that will-you-please-shut-up look. So I did.

But minutes later, when a flock of ducks skid-landed on the lake, I laughed. "Ducks are goofy, huh?"

Mom smiled but not with her eyes, sighed loudly, and replied, "Yep, ducks are goofy." I could tell she really didn't want to talk, but I still did.

"If you want me to stop yakking about her, I'll be quiet."

"You don't have to be quiet, V. If I were you, I'd have lots of questions, too."

Good, I thought, and continued my interrogation—which means to keep asking a person questions they probably don't want to answer. "Why doesn't she care about me?"

"She cares about you, V."

If she cared about me, she would want to know me.

"Then how come I never met her and how come she never calls me and how come I don't get to go to visit her like Daisy gets to visit her grandpa and grandma in Connecticut and how come she doesn't send birthday cards or presents and how come—"

Mom pressed her finger to my lips. "It's because of me, V."

"You mean because she didn't want her son to marry a white woman?"

"Who told you that?"

"I heard you and Gam talking last night."

"What else did you hear?"

"That the accident was your fault . . . Was it?"

Mom hung her head and stammered, "Y-yes. I was driving."

"Were you on your cell phone or something?"

"No, we passed a baby furniture store and there was the prettiest crib in the window, so I made one of my famous U-turns. I can still hear him warning me not to when the truck broadsided us and sent us into the telephone pole. Your dad was gone instantly."

I wanted to get up and run far, far away, but I didn't. "So it really was your fault?"

No wonder Roxanne Diamond was mad. So was I!

"No wonder she hates you!" I blurted out. "If you didn't do that, I would have had a really nice dad! Instead of . . ."

"Instead of what?"

"Instead of just you!" I'd tried very hard not to say that part, but it just flew out and there was no taking it back now.

Mom's eyes filled up with tears. "I made a mistake, Violet. People make mistakes."

"Not just a mistake, a horrible mistake!"

"I'm sorry, Violet," Mom said, and started to cry hard.

Usually always when anyone starts to cry, I feel bad for them, but today I didn't. I was glad she was crying. *I hope she cries enough tears to fill a bathtub,* I thought as I ran to the edge of the lake, peered in, and wished. I wished that she hadn't made the stupid U-turn, I wished that I had a dad, I wished that Roxanne Diamond loved me. I glanced back at her. She was doubled over, weeping. Seeing her like that made me feel sorry for what I had said, and I wished my mom would stop crying. Now.

I went back to where she was still sobbing, sat beside her, and patted her leg.

"I wish you didn't make a U-turn," I whispered.

"So do I."

"But it's not like you meant to, not like murder, right?"

She stared at me with eyes that looked like glass and repeated, "Right. I'm sorry, Violet." Mom took a deep breath and dried her eyes with the sleeve of her shirt.

"I still have some questions. Is it okay to ask them?"

Mom sighed and nodded.

"Is it true that she didn't want him to marry you because you're white?"

"Yes."

"Why?"

"Some black people feel that way."

"And some white people feel that way, too."

"Yes."

"Why?"

"Good question. Many answers, I suppose," she replied.

"Why do people have to come in different colors?" I wondered out loud.

"More beauty that way," Mom answered. "Just imagine if every cat on Earth was a Siamese."

"And none like Hazel?" I asked, picturing a room filled with forty Siamese cats, each an identical replica of the next. "That'd be extremely dull."

Mom reached for my hand and held it. "Exactly."

There was one more thing I needed to know. "Did Gam and Poppy care?"

"About what?"

"About you marrying someone who was black."

"They were hippies."

Hippies? That didn't sound good. "What's a hippie?"

"People from the 1960s and 1970s who believed in peace, love, and happiness—that color didn't matter because we're all humans. It was an era. Gam and Poppy both went to UC Berkeley, lived for a while in a commune . . . and I grew up in Berkeley. People of all colors and every religion were in and out of our house . . . No, they didn't care about your father being black."

"It's too bad Roxanne Diamond wasn't a hippie, huh?"

Mom wiped her tears away and smiled.

I made a wish and took a huge deep breath. "She's having an exhibit of her paintings at the Seattle Art Museum."

"When?"

"Starts next weekend. There's something called a public reception with the artist on Saturday. That means she'll be there?"

"Yes, that's what it means."

"And she can't make us go away because anyone who wants to go to that gallery can?"

"Right."

I took my mom's hand in mine and held it tight. It seemed like a tri-zillion seconds passed before I asked, "Can we go? Maybe she'll like me when she meets me."

And it felt like an eon went by before Mom finally answered.

"Yes. We can."

11

A WEEK OF WAITING

Gam's hairdresser was able to get my hair back to its normal color, and boy, was I glad. Some people just look better with brown hair and I'm definitely one of them. For the first time in a while, I liked what looked back at me from the mirror.

"Can I go to Athena's house? Her mom said it was okay," I asked Gam after we got home.

"No more hair color tricks. Promise?"

"Promise."

"And call me when you get there."

I nodded and sped to Athena's. I couldn't wait to tell her how my life had suddenly become extremely un-boring. Today, there were no clouds in my head, no feeling-sorry-for-myself look on my face.

Athena's mom, Ianthe, opened the door. Her hair is

streaked gold, her eyes greenish blue, and she's usually thin, except for now, because she just had a baby. Ianthe means "violet flower" in Greek, at least that's what she told me a long time ago, so it's kind of like we have the same name. But if you want to know the truth, I actually like the name Violet a lot better. With one arm, she was cradling the baby, who was wrapped tightly in a blanket, and all I could see was the top of his head.

"Hi, Violet," Ianthe whispered.

"Hey, Miz Starros. Can I see him?" I asked.

"Of course, but shhh, he's sleeping," Ianthe replied, carefully peeling the blanket away so I could see his face.

"He's so cute," I said, admiring his dark curls and tiny pink mouth. "Hey, little Dio."

Dio made a baby sound and squirmed.

Like a bullet, Athena flew into the room and ran her hands through my hair. "Your hair is back!" she screeched. "Awesome!"

"Shhh," Athena's mom reminded her.

"All right already," Athena told her as she grabbed my hand and pulled me to her room.

I settled in on her huge pink bean bag chair and got comfy.

"Your mom didn't kill you," she declared.

I waved my arm in front of me as if to say I'm right here and replied, "Do I look dead?"

"You could be a ghost. Maybe I see dead people."

"You're not funny, Athena."

"Yes, I am," she said. She jumped up and did a funny dance to the music that was coming from the TV.

I laughed and shook my head. "You're insane." As usual, it was almost impossible to be anything but happy around Athena, and it's one of the things I liked best about her.

Athena continued dancing until the song ended, then plopped on her bed and started flipping through one of her teen magazines.

"I'm going to Seattle this weekend with my mom. We're staying the whole weekend," I told her.

"For what?"

"To go to an art exhibit."

"Ho-hum," Athena said, and made a fake yawn.

"An exhibit of paintings by my grandmother."

Athena scrunched up her face. "Huh? I never saw her painting anything."

"Not Gam . . . my other grandmother."

"I didn't even know you had another grandmother."

"I do. Her name's Roxanne Kamaria Diamond. And she's famous."

"You are so lying, V."

"I am so not." I reached for her computer. "Turn it on," I commanded. "I'll show you."

I typed in my grandmother's name and showed Athena. "See, Roxanne even has her own website."

Athena studied the photos, glanced at me with a question-mark face, and proclaimed, "But she's black . . . dark black."

"She's my dad's mother. What'd you expect?"

Athena shrugged her shoulders. "I don't know." She stared at the screen and then back at me. "It's just I never think about you really being black."

"But I am black."

"Only half . . . you're biracial."

"Half is still black. What do you think people notice when they first look at me?"

"Curly hair?"

"Not. The first thing they think is Violet Diamond is a *black girl*. In school I'm the only *black girl* in class. And at the ice rink, Yaz Kilroy is the *black girl* who might one day go to Nationals. It's just how people are."

"So? Maybe the first thing people think when they meet me is that I'm Greek."

"Not. People can't tell you're Greek just by looking at you. But people always know when you're black or Asian or Mexican even."

"I spoze," she replied.

"How would you feel if you were the only white girl in class?" I asked.

Athena shrugged. "I don't know. I've never been the only one," she answered, then glanced back at the pictures of Roxanne Diamond on the computer screen. "Her clothes look like she's from Africa."

"No, she's bohemian."

"Where's that?"

"It just means she's different. And look at her paintings . . . they're really good, huh?"

Athena nodded. "Can I go with you? I know my mom'll let me. Anything is better than being told to shush all day long because the baby is sleeping or listening to him cry, even in the middle of the night. Plus, I'm being forced to learn Greek cooking from scratch from my grandma every day. *Microwave* isn't in her vocabulary. Yesterday we made stuffed grape leaves."

I'd eaten stuffed grape leaves before and they were really good. "Yummy."

"I know they taste good, but I hate cooking. Please take me with you."

"Um . . ."

"Um, what?"

"I don't think my mom will like that."

"Why?" Athena asked.

I felt embarrassed to tell her the truth, but I did. "Because I've never even met my other grandmother before."

"How come?"

A knock on the door kept me from spilling the beans.

"Come in," Athena said.

It was Athena's grandma, Mrs. Matsoukis. I've met her lots of times. She has a foreign accent, mostly gray hair, a happy round face, but a slim body. "Athena, I am making meat and macaroni pie. Pastitsio. It's a good dish. You should learn."

"But my friend is here. It'll take all day," Athena whined.

I waved. "Hi, Mrs. Matsoukis."

"Hello, Violet. You should learn, too, and join us for dinner."

I'd never had meat and macaroni pie, but it sure sounded good. "Does it have cheese?" I asked.

"Kefalotiri cheese."

Athena rolled her eyes. "Gramma, I really hate to cook."

"But you like to eat. Come."

As instructed, we followed Mrs. Matsoukis to the kitchen. "First, the meat sauce."

I really like to cook and it must have shown, because Athena's grandma patted me on the back as I carefully mixed the meat sauce in the pan. "You are good at this, Violet. Do you cook with your mother or grandmother?"

"Sometimes I make lasagna or spaghetti with my grandma. Italian food is her specialty, but mostly my poppy does the cooking. He's the gourmet. He even takes cooking classes. Last night he cooked spicy-sweet tangerine shrimp with bok choy and rice."

"On Sunday, we are having a party to celebrate the

arrival of Dio Starros. You will come," Mrs. Matsoukis commanded.

"Thank you, but I can't. I'm going to Seattle."

"To meet her other grandmother for the first time," Athena informed her.

"Other grandmother?" Mrs. Matsoukis asked.

"My black grandmother. I'm biracial."

"What is this 'biracial'?"

"It means she's two races . . . half black race and half white race," Athena replied.

Mrs. Matsoukis popped a cherry tomato in her mouth and chewed. "Aren't we all human race, Violet?"

I stopped stirring. "Yes, but . . ."

She didn't let me finish. "Of course we are. Human race comes in many colors. This word 'biracial' is silly talk."

"Is that what people think in Greece, that we're all the same?" I asked.

"In Greece, no, but in my mind, yes. No more silly talk . . . understand?"

Athena and I stared at each other and smiled. "Got it."

Athena was right, the meat and macaroni pie did take hours. Finally, when we were done, we mixed the rest of the grated cheese with bread crumbs, sprinkled them over the top, and put the meat pie in the oven.

And while it was baking, Athena and I went back to

her room, where I finally spilled most of the beans about my mom and Roxanne Diamond. There were only two secrets I didn't tell her—the one about my grandmother not wanting my father to marry my mom because she was white and the one about my mom making the U-turn.

Those facts I decided to keep to myself.

12

MORE SLOW MOTION

At dawn the next morning, loudmouthed Hazel started up. She was mewing her *I'm hungry and you need to feed me now* mew. But my eyes were sealed shut and my body wouldn't move. I needed more sleep. "Later," I told her.

"Meow! Meow! Meow!"

And right then, for the first time, I wished Hazel would disappear, not forever but just for a little while so I could stay comfy in my bed.

"Meow!"

My head felt glued to the pillow. "I'm sleepy," I groaned.

But because cats don't seem to understand English, Hazel kept mewing.

"All right, you win." I squiggled out of bed, practically

sleepwalked into the kitchen, and was opening a can of cat food when Poppy came in through the back door, toting his golf clubs.

In an instant, Hazel dashed for the door, and before Poppy could close it, she squeezed outside.

"No!"

Poppy and I ran after her, but she leaped and sprinted off like she was happy to be free.

"Come back, Hazel!" I yelled.

Suddenly Poppy grabbed my hand and stopped in his tracks. "No sense in chasing something that doesn't want to be caught," he said as he put his arm around my shoulder and led me back to the house. "Sorry, V."

I hung my head and whimpered, "It's not your fault, Poppy, it's mine . . . for wishing."

"Wishing?" Poppy asked.

"That Hazel would vanish for a little while so I could go back to sleep."

"I don't think wishing had anything to do with it. It's what cats do, V. She'll be back," he promised. "Put the food right outside the door and we'll wait."

We put two chairs by the door and sat.

"I'll just wish for her to come back," I told him, and made a silent wish.

Poppy frowned. "This wishing business of yours has me a little concerned."

"Why?" I asked. "Wishes can come true."

"Sometimes . . . but other things just are, like a cat that's used to being outside making a break for it when a door opens . . . a simple case of a highly probable event." Before Poppy retired, he was a professor. "And one that's likely to keep occurring," he added, "like a drop of rain landing right on the tip of your nose during a storm."

I chimed in, "Unless you do something to stop it, like carrying an umbrella."

"Righto, my dear. So if we put a sign on the door that says 'be careful not to let Hazel get out,' that might reduce the probability of her escaping regularly. We need to *do* something to keep it from being a highly probable event."

I understood. "Instead of just wishing, righto?"

"Righto," he echoed.

I dashed to my room for paper, a marker, and some tape. Then, just as Poppy and I finished making the sign, I heard the tinkling of the bell on her collar. And when she crept up to the food, we scooted her inside.

"Bad Hazel," I scolded.

She looked up from the food and softly meowed as if she were apologizing.

"Speaking of food, you hungry, V?" Poppy asked.

"Yes."

"Eggs Benedict sound good?" he asked.

I was ravenous and not in the mood to wait for a fancy breakfast. "How about just plain eggs and bacon?"

"I hear you're going to an art show this weekend," Poppy commented as he cooked.

"Mom told you?"

Poppy nodded.

"Did you ever meet her?"

He sighed and replied, "Only once."

"At their wedding?"

"No, she didn't make it to the wedding. I met her at your father's funeral."

"She was sad, huh?"

"We were all sad, Violet. We were all very sad," he whispered.

"But she was his mother and he was her only child, not like you and Gam, who have three children, so she was probably more sad, right?"

Poppy scrunched his eyebrows together and disagreed. "The loss of any child, whether an only child or one of ten, would make a parent very sad, Violet."

"But if you had other children, then you'd still have someone else to love."

He frowned. "One child can't replace another."

"But—"

Poppy interrupted, "I think you have to be a parent to understand." Suddenly, that same stung-by-a-bee look that Mom gets covered Poppy's face.

That look is *usually always* my clue to change the

subject, so I did. "I made my first Axel at the rink the other day . . . without falling."

Poppy slid the plate of bacon and scrambled eggs in front of me, finally smiled, gave me two thumbs-up, and said, "Bravo, V . . . bravo."

13

AFRICA

Just when you want the days to zoom by like a go-kart or roller coaster, they slow down like those kiddie pony rides at the state fair.

Athena was going to be gone all day with her mom for the new baby's doctor's appointments and stuff, and I wasn't in the mood to ice-skate with Yaz, so I pulled out the atlas and my notebook of *Places Violet Diamond Will Travel to Someday*. I opened the atlas and flipped to the Africa pages. Africa is a humungous continent and we'd studied it a little in geography class, but I didn't really know much about it and I'd never, ever thought about going there.

From the atlas, I learned that Africa has more countries than the United States has states, fifty-four in all.

It also said it has a little more than 20 percent of the Earth's land and the longest river, the Nile. I looked at the countries and wrote down some that had names I liked the sound of. Later, I'd look them up online. In my notebook, I scribbled *Cameroon, Kenya, Botswana,* and *Mozambique.* That seemed like a pretty good start. If Roxanne Diamond was Afrocentric, I figured it would be good if I knew at least a little bit about Africa. That way, we'd have something to talk about—I mean, if she would even talk to me.

The insides of me, where my heart beats, hoped she would.

Studying Africa ate up the whole day, and by dinnertime my body was hungry and my brain was full of interesting facts.

While helping Gam make lasagna, I began filling her up with information about the African continent. "Did you know Africa has, like, fifty-four countries?"

"Yes, V. Parts of Africa are so beautiful," Gam said with a starry-eyed look.

"You've been there?" I asked.

"Yes, Poppy and I went on a safari in Kenya. It was an amazing experience," she replied.

"For real? How come you never talked about it before?" I asked.

"You never asked before."

As I'd learned online, not everything about Africa was good. "But a lot of kids are starving and sick and don't have doctors," I told her. "And that's pretty sad, huh?"

"No, it's very sad."

As Gam drained the lasagna noodles, the steam fogged her glasses and for a minute she was blind. We both laughed. I thought about Roxanne Diamond and wondered if she made lasagna and wore glasses. Part of me started to think maybe it was a mistake to go to Seattle. Maybe I was chasing someone who really didn't want to be caught.

But I have to meet her. I just have to.

14

SEATTLE, HERE WE COME

"Do you think I should wear a dress?" I asked my mom as I searched through the clothes in my closet. Tomorrow morning, we were leaving for Seattle.

She was sitting on my bed, wearing blue doctor scrubs and a worried look. "It's up to you, V."

My hand landed on a lavender and purple striped dress and I pulled it out. It was pretty and girly but not too fancy. "Perfect?" I asked.

"Perfect," she said, but tears were in her eyes.

Sometimes a person needs another person to hold their hand, at least that's what Gam says. And I could tell by the look in my mom's eyes that she needed hers held—now.

I snuggled beside her on the bed and took her hand.

"We don't have to go if it makes you sad. I mean, it really doesn't matter that much to me," I told her, but it wasn't the truth. More than anything, I wanted to go.

But if you say no, I will give you the silent treatment for months.

"I talked it over with one of the psychologists at work, and we both wonder if it's a good idea. I don't want you to be rejected or disappointed and have your feelings hurt, Violet."

"You mean maybe she won't talk to us?"

"That could happen. She didn't say a word to me at your father's funeral . . . wouldn't even look at me. It was as if I'd died, too. I just want to warn you. If she does that to us tomorrow, we will leave right away and I don't want any argument from you, understood?"

She won't do that to me. I didn't make a U-turn.

I squeezed her hand tightly. "Understood."

She kissed my cheek and said good night, but she still had a worrywart face.

I showered, washed my hair, towel dried it, did finger curls, and put in bobby pins because I was desperate to look pretty tomorrow.

Later, Hazel was huddled beside me and my head was on the pillow, but I was wide-awake, staring at the dark ceiling, when my door opened and Daisy crept in. "V?" she whispered. "You asleep?"

"Not." I sat up and turned on the table lamp.

D plopped on the bed. "I just came to say *bonne chance* tomorrow. Good luck."

"Good luck? It's not a test or a spelling bee or anything like that, Daisy."

"I just meant I hope she's nice to you."

"Me too," I replied.

Daisy gently patted my head, and right then, I felt good. Good like when you press your nose into the middle of a gardenia and sniff out all the sweet smell.

"Meeting her might be weird, huh?" I said.

Daisy shrugged. "Maybe . . . but I think it might be good for you to know her."

"Do you think it'll be like finally getting to meet your birth mother?" I asked.

"Mom is your birth mother, goofball. It's not the same, V."

"But I still have another family I don't really know about. Don't you understand?"

Daisy shook her head. "I guess not really."

"Because you know your whole family," I explained. "But if you had a grandmother you'd never met, wouldn't you want to meet her?"

She smiled and said, "Yeah, I would."

"So now you get it?" I asked again.

"I do," Daisy said. "Plus, since your dad adopted me, I suppose she's sort of my grandmother, too, right?"

"Wow, I never thought about that. Humph. You get three grandmothers and I only get two. Not fair."

Daisy giggled. "Not fair, but true."

Something about that made me shrink a little, and the sweet smell of the gardenia Daisy had brought into my room went poof. What I felt right then was something I had never felt before, but I knew exactly which word from my word book fit the feeling—bewildered.

Daisy kissed my forehead, said, "Sweet dreams, li'l sis. *Je t'aime*," and before I could reply, she had quietly shut my door and was gone.

I turned off the light and my head sank into the pillow again. I cuddled Hazel and thought, *Roxanne Diamond belongs to Daisy, too?* For what felt like a very long time, I stared into the night.

I don't want to share her—yet.

Seattle is only a car ride away from Moon Lake, so we go there a few times a year. It's where my mom, dad, and Daisy lived before I was born. I love Seattle. The countryside was every shade of green and the sun was shining its light in my eyes.

As usual, Mom was listening to her public radio station, so I listened to my iPod. It seemed like the car was rolling along to the beat of my music when I yawned. What is it about long car rides that makes sleep show up?

Maybe I need some fresh air, I thought, and rolled down the window.

"No open windows on the freeway, V. You know that. Close it now."

I'd forgotten the *no open windows on the freeway because stuff can fly in and stick in your eye or something* rule.

"If you're hot, I'll turn on the air."

"I'm not hot." Seconds later, I yawned again and started to nod off.

Certain things seem to be unstoppable—Yaz once she starts a spin, a fall on the ice at the rink when someone bumps into you hard, and a nap when you hardly slept a wink the night before.

No matter what I did, sleep wouldn't give up, and in seconds I went from half asleep to all the way.

Sometime later, I squirmed, stretched, and woke up. In seconds, my eyes landed on the Space Needle. We were in downtown Seattle.

15

IN SEATTLE

I love fancy hotels. I love room service and towels that are always fluffy and beds that get made for you and chocolate candies on your pillow at night and indoor swimming pools. I just do. In fact, I was thinking just the other day that being in charge of a fancy hotel might be a very cool job.

We pulled up to the extremely fancy hotel where we stayed the last time we were in Seattle, and two guys in burgundy valet suits opened the doors of our car. The reception at the gallery wasn't until six p.m., so we had time just to be.

"Can we order room service?" I asked my mom before the bellhop had even closed the room door.

"Yes," Mom answered.

I bounced on the soft bed and yelled, "Yay!"

Mom and I pigged out on soup and sandwiches and salad and dessert and were watching her favorite movie, *The Wizard of Oz*, on an old movie channel, when she nodded off.

I turned off the TV and stared out the window at the city below. Cars sped by and all kinds of people strolled along. A runner dashing across the street nearly got hit by a car, and the driver honked twice. A dog yanked its owner down the sidewalk, and four people on bicycles held up traffic while a blind man, wearing sunglasses, moved his long white cane with a red tip from side to side. At that moment, I decided that I prefer city life. And when I grow up, I'm going to live in a very big city where there are all people of all colors, maybe New York, not some humdrum small town. Maybe I'll be bohemian. Yep, definitely bohemian.

By three thirty Mom was wide-awake and pulling on her tennis shoes. "Let's go for a walk. We have plenty of time."

First, we stopped in Neptune Music Company, where Mom bought an original Jimi Hendrix vinyl album. Then we searched the racks at a vintage dress store, where Mom bought a navy blue silk suit from the 1950s. She's seriously into vintage clothes, and I have to admit it looked pretty good on her.

"Can we move to Seattle?" I asked. "I like it here. It's so much fun and there are lots of different kinds of people."

"Maybe we should," she replied.

"Huh? Are you serious?"

"Yes. Moon Lake is so . . . isolated from the real world. If I can find a good job. Once Daisy graduates. It wouldn't be fair to her right now."

"Yeah," I agreed. "But are you really serious?"

She gently squeezed my hand. "Yes, Violet, I am."

At that point, I stopped looking around Seattle with visitor's eyes, trying to see everything in a flash, soaking up all the sights and sounds, storing them in my memory. My eyes now saw the city like a person who might live there one day, a person with plenty of time.

We were browsing inside another store at toys and cards and posters and stuff when Mom's cell phone sounded off the alarm tone. She grabbed my hand and together we speed-walked back to the hotel. Like a candle, time had melted away, the way it always seems to when you're having fun.

Mom took a shower first.

"Your turn, V . . . and make it a quickie." I put on the shower cap because my curls were looking extremely perfect and I didn't want them to frizz up the way they do when there's steam or fog around.

By the time I came out of the bathroom, Mom was dressed in the suit she'd just bought and she was wearing makeup, even lip gloss. "Wow! You look pretty," I told her.

"Thank you," she replied as she sniffed her clothes.

"It kind of has that old-clothes smell. Maybe I shouldn't wear it before I send it to the cleaners."

I got close to her and took a long whiff. "I don't smell anything."

Mom squinted at me. "You swear?"

Just to be sure, I took another sniff. "I swear."

"Okay, hurry and get dressed."

We drove up to the museum at exactly 6:05. My insides felt squirmy like worms wiggling and my hands were sweaty. I got out of the car, straightened out my clothes, and fluffed up my hair. "How do I look?"

Mom smiled, even with her eyes, and answered, "Beautiful, V. You look beautiful."

Beautiful? I don't think anyone had ever called me beautiful before.

"My little girl is growing up," Mom added.

"Do you think I'll ever be *breathtaking*, like Daisy?"

"Absolutely."

Suddenly, I felt amazing and spectacular, sparkly like a diamond.

16

MEET ROXANNE DIAMOND

For a moment we stood at the entrance to the museum, where mom reminded me about what we were going to do if Roxanne Diamond ignored us.

"I remember," I told her. "If she won't talk to us, we're going to leave."

"And no argument, promise?"

"Promise . . . can we please go inside now?"

Mom held my hand and took a really deep breath, then we entered through the double doors.

Inside the huge room that had a polished concrete floor, the paintings of Roxanne Diamond covered the walls, and there were white people, black people, and all sorts of other people holding wineglasses, talking, and eating hors d'oeuvres, and I, Violet Diamond, for the first time in my life, felt kind of grown up.

My eyes searched the room until I finally saw the back of someone who had gray dreadlocks and was wearing a dress made from African material just like on the website. There were people huddled around the woman. It had to be her.

I tore away from my mom and bolted. In seconds I was standing in front of Roxanne Diamond. Her skin was the color of chocolate and she had brown eyes like mine. She wasn't fat or skinny. She was just right and she had on red lipstick.

Patiently, I waited for her to notice me, but she was so busy talking that she didn't. Inside my chest, my heart was pounding fast.

Am I invisible or something? I'm right here, Violet Roxanne Diamond.

Finally, I tugged on her dress. "I'm Violet," I blurted.

The people in the group around her smiled, but Roxanne Diamond looked at me like she didn't believe what she was seeing.

"Your granddaughter," I added.

And that was when the faces of the people around her changed to curious.

Just like I'd practiced for the past week, I reached out my hand for her to shake and Roxanne Diamond took it and held it. She stared at me in an odd way, like she was trying to memorize me. But when my mom got to my side, Roxanne Diamond immediately let go of my hand and her look changed to not-so-nice.

"Hello, Roxanne," Mom said, and offered her hand.

I could tell Roxanne didn't want to shake my mom's hand, but because there were people around, she did, giving my mom a counterfeit smile.

"Justine. How nice that you could make it."

Somehow, those words made the faces of the people who were standing around turn normal again. One by one they drifted away, as if they could tell we needed some privacy.

Finally, when it was just the three of us, I told her something else I'd practiced. "Don't be mad at my mom, okay? Because I made her bring me."

That made her almost smile. "You made her bring you, huh?"

"Yep. I found out about this exhibit online and I wanted to meet you and see your paintings . . . so here we are."

"So here you are," Roxanne replied.

Is that all she has to say?

I was expecting hugs and twenty kisses and lots of mushy things. But at least she was talking to us, which meant my mom wasn't going to drag me outside and screech away in the car.

She looked my mom over good, from her hair and face clear down to her shoes. "You're looking well, Justine."

"So are you, Roxanne," Mom said.

Neither one was smiling, but boy, they were sure being polite.

Thinking this might possibly be the only time I would ever get to talk to her, I said a bunch of stuff in one breath. "Your paintings are really cool and you look just as pretty as your picture and I like the clothes you wear and the way you're a bohemian."

"A bohemian?"

"Yeah. Like you have an unconventional life."

Her gaze shifted from me to Mom.

Right then, a flock of people gathered around Roxanne Diamond, some just wanting to shake her hand while others praised her artwork, and suddenly Mom and I were pushed out of the circle.

"Don't leave," Roxanne told my mom.

Don't leave?

I smiled.

Mom nodded as if to say okay, and we wandered off to look at the paintings.

Some of them were on canvasses so ginormous that I wondered how they got them inside the room. I asked Mom, but she said she didn't know much about art.

"That's okay," I told her. "Probably most artists don't know much about being a doctor."

For the first time since we got there, Mom smiled.

Most of the paintings were of real people and real

things, but there were three that I couldn't figure out. I stopped in front of one. "The colors are pretty, but what do you think it's supposed to be?" I asked my mom as I chomped on an appetizer.

"Hmm . . . I don't know. It's abstract."

"In English, please."

"It's whatever you think it is or want it to be."

"Actually, it's a representation of the labyrinth of the human mind," a voice spoke up from behind us. The voice of Roxanne Diamond.

And I thought my mom didn't speak English.

I stepped back from the painting and gave her a side glance. "Huh?"

"Sometimes the inner workings of the human mind are so convoluted, it makes it hard to find our way," Roxanne explained.

It was one of those times—time to change the conversation fast—and I knew how. "Should I call you Grandma?"

I didn't expect it to, but that shut her up. By the look on her face, you would have thought I'd asked her for a million dollars.

"Is that what you want to call me?"

"No," I replied. "I could call you RD."

"For Roxanne Diamond."

"Yep. But I also like your middle name, Kamaria, because it means 'like the moon' . . . that's kind of awesome."

"You've done your research," she said.

"Yep. Research is something I'm very good at."

That was when she finally gave me the grandparent-love look. I knew because it's the same look I get from Gam and Poppy. But all of sudden the look turned sad and her eyes got watery with tears. Carefully, she wiped them away before they could drip onto her cheeks.

"What's the matter?" I asked.

She patted my head and whispered, "You remind me too much of your father."

"Sorry," I told her. "I didn't mean to."

But my words didn't stop Roxanne from crying. And as I glanced around the room, I noticed a few people watching us.

My mom reached out to touch her shoulder, but Roxanne jerked away and angrily said, "Coming here was a mistake, Justine."

Right then, without warning, a swarm of fans surrounded Roxanne Diamond and swallowed her up. I reached for her but my mom caught my hand, and the next thing I knew we were outside, standing on the sidewalk.

Mom was shaking her head the way she does when she's mad. "I knew this would happen! I knew it!"

"Sorry," I repeated.

"There's nothing for you to be sorry for, V," she said, then hugged me so tight, I could barely breathe.

Mom led me to the car, and during the drive back to the hotel, the worst gloomy clouds ever filled up my brain. I gazed out the window at the city lights. Roxanne had turned Seattle ugly, and like a violet, I shrank again.

"I hate Seattle," I told my mom. "It's not so great. Maybe we could move to Portland. Portland's pretty, don't you think?"

"Portland might be nice," she said sadly.

"Or really far away, like New York City."

Mom sighed. "New York's nice, too."

Or maybe if there were people on the moon, we could move there and never have to think about Roxanne Diamond again.

The problem was, I knew I wasn't going to be able to erase her from my mind.

I turned my head away from my mom and, as quietly as I could, cried.

Too sad + very mad = lots of tears.

17

BAD WISHES

We hadn't eaten dinner, so we stopped at Serious Pie for some pizza, but I wasn't very hungry and the food, because I was feeling sad, didn't taste very good—well, maybe the pepperoni and mushrooms did, because pepperoni and mushrooms always taste good.

"So much for my wishes," I said.

Mom patted my hand. "Sounds to me like you're praying, Violet, not wishing. When we wish, it's usually for something frivolous."

"Frivolous?" A new word.

"Something not serious. Like what you want for your birthday. Prayers are for more serious things," Mom said.

"Like?"

"Like at night when I pray for you and Daisy to be safe or when I pray for the sick babies in the nursery."

"But Daisy told me you're mad at God," I told her.

"Mad doesn't mean I stopped believing. There are just some things I don't understand." She sighed loudly.

"There are some things I don't understand, either—like why Roxanne Diamond acted the way she did. And that's probably why, on the way here, I wished something bad," I confessed.

"What?"

"I wished Roxanne Diamond would be sad and cry . . . a lot. That's bad, huh?"

"Prayers and wishes should always be good, but we all think bad thoughts when our feelings get hurt. It's human, V. And about what happened with Roxanne, I blame myself. I should have listened to my inner voice when it warned me that coming here wasn't a good idea."

If Mom was blaming herself, I figured I could, too. "Maybe if you hadn't been there, she . . . ," I blurted, then shut my lips tight to keep any more words from flying out.

"She what?" Mom asked.

"Never mind," I said. "And please don't get that stung-by-a-bee look on your face. I really hate it when you do that."

"Stung-by-a-bee look?"

"Yep. That look you get when you're mad or your

feelings get hurt or you don't want to talk about something. It's what you always do . . . and Poppy does it, too. It's like a warning not to say anything that's not nice."

For some reason, that made her start laughing—hard—and for a long time. And soon, I started giggling, too. It was as if we'd caught a disease, the laughing disease.

The silence that came after the laughing spell made me kind of nervous, so I broke it. "Maybe we should just go back to the way it was before . . . when she was kind of dead."

"But she's not dead, V."

"If she doesn't want to have anything to do with us, then it's kind of like she doesn't exist, so we should pretend she's dead. That way we won't have to be sad about her. And I promise not to make any more good wishes or prayers about seeing her."

"Or bad ones?"

I stared into my mother's hazel eyes for what felt like a long time before I answered, "Or bad ones."

18

ANOTHER SWERVE

The next morning, we ordered room service and had a very yummy breakfast, which included French toast, my favorite. And afterward, we lounged on the beds for a while, Mom reading a book, me playing games on my iPad but mostly thinking.

I don't need Roxanne Kamaria Diamond making me feel like an unwanted guest, some kind of party crasher.

I glanced over at my mom and smiled. She loves me. Plus, Gam and Poppy and Daisy do, too. That I knew for sure.

And eventually, checkout time snuck up on us and we had to hustle.

Hurriedly, we exited the elevator and headed to the lobby.

That's when we saw her, standing there as still as a statue, wearing dark sunglasses, black pants, and a white tunic blouse—Roxanne Diamond, looking not so bohemian.

We halted and Roxanne, with a sorry look on her face, approached us.

I took my mom's hand and tried to pull her in another direction, but it was no use and in seconds Roxanne was up close.

"How'd you know where to find us?" I asked.

"I called the house and your grandmother told me," Roxanne answered calmly, then removed her sunglasses. Her eyes were puffy and red like when someone has cried a bunch. "I'm sorry," she said, and sighed. "I just wasn't expecting this."

"Neither were we, Roxanne," Mom told her.

"It's just that *she* reminds me so much of Warren, and all the pain came flooding back."

She? I'm not she, I'm Violet. And I'm your granddaughter and you're supposed to be nice to me.

Mom glanced at her watch. "We need to check out, Roxanne, unless there's something else."

Roxanne touched Mom's arm. "Can we start fresh, Justine? I'd like to try."

"I don't want *her* feelings hurt again, Roxanne."

Her? Why do they keep talking about me like I'm not here?

"What happened yesterday made her cry," Mom added.

"It made me cry, too," she admitted.

As Mom paid the bill, Roxanne stood nearby, and when we left the hotel, she followed us outside. She didn't seem the same as she did yesterday, famous and beautiful, lighting up the museum. Today, Roxanne Diamond seemed normal, tired, and small.

"Justine, unless you're in a hurry, I was hoping we might grab a bite to eat," she said.

Mom glanced my way as if to ask how I felt.

I shrugged and said truthfully, "My stomach's still full from breakfast."

"How about a walk or a coffee?" Roxanne offered.

Mom stuffed our suitcases in the trunk and replied, "Sure."

"We could go to Pike Place Market," I said as we strolled along. "It's not that far. Or we could go to the Space Needle, but I don't think they have coffee. Did you know Seattle is called the Emerald City, just like in *The Wizard of Oz*?" Mostly to fill up the quiet, but partly because I was nervous, I was being a chatterbox.

"Pike Place Market sounds good. I haven't had my morning coffee yet," Roxanne said.

Mom agreed, and we headed to Pike Street.

Roxanne ordered espresso, Mom had a decaf vanilla latte, and I had my favorite, a caramel apple spice. And as we sat sipping, except for the sounds all around us, there was more silence.

Someone say something, please.

"How's your work at the hospital, Justine?" Roxanne finally asked. "You're still working with newborns, aren't you?"

"She's the head of the NICU," I bragged. "The neonatal intensive care unit," I added, in case she didn't know.

"How wonderful that must be," Roxanne Diamond said, smiling like she really meant it.

"It's rewarding, sometimes a challenge, some days it's heartbreaking. I've worked very hard to make it a top-notch unit."

"Drive and work ethic . . . two qualities I respect," Roxanne commented. "Warren was the same."

Mom's eyes got misty. "I know."

After that, Mom chatted about her doctor work and Roxanne rambled on about hers, and by the time they'd finished their drinks, it seemed like they were all talked out. It felt the same way it does when the teacher makes you work on a project with someone you barely know and all you have in common is the project.

"We could go to the shops," I said. "They have a 3-D puzzle store."

But before we got up to leave, Roxanne reached in her purse, pulled out an envelope, and handed it to my mom. "Before we go, I have a letter I'd like you to read, Justine."

Mom took the envelope and read the three-page letter. By the time she finished, there were tears in her eyes.

"I hope that explains some things," Roxanne told her.

"It does. Thank you for telling me," Mom said as she carefully folded the letter and placed it in the envelope. The way she did it reminded me of the way she treats my Mother's Day cards, as if it was something nice, a thing worth saving.

What did it say?

We had looked around a lot in the 3-D puzzle store, rummaged through the antique place, and headed into Holy Cow Records. A place we *usually always* go to whenever we come to Seattle.

"My mom's really into old stuff, especially records," I told Roxanne.

"So am I," she replied. "I have quite a few."

Quietly, we were going through the store's collection when Roxanne broke the silence. She stammered a bit, then said, "I have to stay in Seattle until next weekend, but then I have two weeks off between shows, and I was hoping Violet could fly with me back to Los Angeles for a week. If you don't have other plans."

Stuff inside my brain felt jumbled up like in Roxanne's human mind painting. Part of me wanted to go back to pretending she was some kind of strange extinct animal. But most of me wanted to spend some time with this person whose eyes were kind.

I tugged Mom's sleeve. "I wanna go."

Mom nodded and said, "Okay."

19

MY TURN

"What'd the letter say?" I asked as we drove home. "Can I read it?"

"It's about grown-up things," she answered.

"But you could tell me some of it, couldn't you?"

"Part of it talked about a letter she'd written to me a long time ago, apologizing for how she'd acted toward me, especially for not coming to the wedding, and how she was so excited about the baby. How she had wanted to reconcile."

Reconcile? Another new one for my word book. "What's that mean?"

"She wanted to become friends."

"So where's the letter? Do you have it?"

"No, she never mailed it," Mom said.

"Why not?" I asked.

"The day she wrote it was the day of the accident," Mom replied sadly.

"Oh," I replied. What else could I say?

So, that's why she's letting me go to Los Angeles with Roxanne.

We'd only been home for an hour, and I was busy cleaning out Hazel's smelly litter box, when Athena came over.

"So?" she asked as she plopped on my bed.

"So I'm leaving this coming Saturday to go to Los Angeles to stay at her house for a week."

"No way. Are you flying alone?"

"Not. Mom's driving me back to Seattle and Roxanne and I are taking the plane together."

"Why are you calling her Roxanne? Isn't she your grandma?"

"Yep," I replied, "but I didn't decide what I should call her yet."

"Are you gonna go see the Hollywood sign and the Walk of Fame and go to Malibu and Disneyland and Universal City? Because if you are, you have to take me with you."

"I don't think so—not this time, Athena. I mean, I don't really know her at all, but I don't think she'd say yes."

Athena poked out her lip and frowned.

"I promise to take lots of pictures, though."

"Okay, and then when we're old . . . like, eighteen . . . we can go there together, promise?"

I grinned and nodded.

We went to the kitchen to raid the fridge, and Daisy and Wyatt were already there. They were speaking French to each other. When they do, both Athena and I wonder what they're saying, but we figure it's mushy stuff because of the way their eyes get that dreamy-romantic look. When it happens when I'm alone it's just plain embarrassing, but when Athena's there she starts clowning around, making it funny.

"*Bonjour, petites* dude-ettes, good to see you," Wyatt said.

"Hey, Wyatt," Athena and I replied at the same time.

When Wyatt kissed Daisy on the tip of her nose, Athena began making imaginary kisses into the air, and said, "Ooh-la-la, lovebirds!" I tried hard to keep the giggles inside my mouth, but they came out anyway.

Daisy rolled her eyes at us. "*Petits enfants.* I forgot there were such *little children* here," she said.

Wyatt put two fingers in his mouth and whistled loudly. "Chillax, females!" We all cracked up.

Daisy joined Athena in the refrigerator raid and asked, "So how was the art show, V?"

"Fine," I told her. Later, when we were alone, I'd tell her the whole story, but not now. "Plus we went to Serious Pie."

"Lucky Violet," Daisy said.

Right then, Athena, with her big mouth, broke my big news. "And she's going to Los Angeles on Saturday and Disneyland and Hollywood and maybe even Malibu," she blabbed.

"What!" Daisy shrieked.

"Awesome, little dude-ette!" Wyatt shouted.

Part of me didn't want to straighten this out, but I knew I had to. Otherwise, the story was going to get bigger and bigger and bigger. "I never said we were going to Disneyland or Hollywood or Malibu, but I am going to Los Angeles for a whole week."

"No way! I wanna go," D whined like a kid begging for a toy.

I never got to go to Connecticut with Daisy. Now everyone wants to have a piece of my excitement. It's my turn.

"Maybe next time," I said with a big grin.

"C'est la vie," Wyatt said to Daisy.

And with that, the four of us began to devour the food.

Day by day, like the food on the table, the boring pieces of my life were being swallowed up.

20

SOONER THAN I THOUGHT

That night, Daisy came into my room and sat in one of her yoga poses on the floor. "So tell me."

"Everything? It's a lot."

"Everything."

After I'd rattled off the whole story, Daisy shook her head as if she couldn't believe her ears. "And after all that, you still want to go to her house?"

"She apologized, D. And she was crying," I said in Roxanne's defense. "I thought you'd be happy for me."

Daisy got up and sat close beside me on the bed. "I am," she said. "Really."

I can't say why at that moment I wondered if Daisy knew the truth about the accident, but I suppose that's why it's called wondering, because it kind of comes

99

unexpectedly, the same way curiosity does. "Did you know Mom was driving when they had the accident?" I asked.

"Yeah, I knew."

"But did you know that Mom made a—"

Daisy finished the question for me. "A U-turn?"

"Yeah, a U-turn."

Daisy nodded.

"How come you never told me?"

Daisy shrugged. "Seemed like it might weird you out." She paused, then asked, "Did it?"

I picked nervously at my fingernails. "Yeah, it did." And that was when I cried.

Daisy hugged my shoulder and nuzzled me. "Try not to think about that stuff, V. Try to think about having a good time in LA, promise . . . *promets*?"

I leaned into my sister's shoulder. "Okay, promise."

Once Daisy was gone, I pulled out my notebook of *Places Violet Diamond Will Travel to Someday*.

After *Los Angeles, California,* which I'd written in months ago, I added: *And sooner than I thought.* Then I numbered 1–7 for seven days.

Places I'd like to go to while I'm in Los Angeles, California, with Roxanne Diamond, also known as RC, also known as Grandma, or maybe even Kamaria.

1. Disneyland, of course
2. Universal Studios, possibly
3. Santa Monica Beach, I think
4. Hollywood, definitely
5. Malibu
6. ?
7. ?

Because I figured there were places other than the ones I'd thought up where she'd want to take me, I left two days with question marks. I closed my notebook and climbed into bed. I was really tired, and lucky for me, I nodded off fast.

21

COUNTDOWN

It was my day to golf with Poppy, but he had a dental appointment. And as far as I knew, Athena was still getting daily cooking lessons and I wasn't in the mood to spend all day in anyone's kitchen, but I didn't want to stay home, either, so I asked Gam to drop me off at the rink.

There are days when Gam gets quiet. She calls those her moody days, and I thought maybe this was one of them, because she was hardly talking as we drove. But I wondered if it had something to do with Roxanne and what happened in Seattle. Everyone seemed a little different since Mom and I got back.

"What's the matter?" I asked.

"Nothing. Everything is fine. Just a lot on my mind."

"With your online business?"

Gam nodded.

I knew Mom had told her about my trip to Los Angeles, but I decided to talk about it anyway. "I'm leaving on Saturday for Los Angeles with Roxanne."

"Your mother told me. I expect you'll have a wonderful time."

"I hope so. You're not mad about that, are you?"

She gave me a side glance. "Of course not. I'll just miss you."

"Oh, Gam, it's only a week. I'll be back before you know it."

"She's a very interesting person, isn't she?"

"Yep, unconventional."

Gam chuckled. "Not like boring old me."

So that was it. "You're not that boring," I told her. "Plus you're extremely nice."

That made her smile. "Not that boring, huh?"

"Most grown-ups are boring, Gam, not just you. Mom is boring, especially when she talks doctor talk. Even Poppy's boring. I bet even Daisy'll be boring and Wyatt will be double boring. I mean, he's already boring."

"But you probably won't be boring, right?" Gam asked.

"Probably not," I replied.

That made her giggle.

When we reached the rink, Gam took my hand in

hers and said, "I suppose when you don't know about the other part of your family, it feels like there's something missing. Like all of the pieces of the puzzle aren't there."

Gam had put my feelings into words.

"Exactly," I told her.

She squeezed my hand tightly. "I really hope you find those pieces, V. And I especially want you to have a good time."

"I'm not gone yet," I reminded her.

"I know, but I just needed to say that. Pick you up at three. Wait inside, promise?"

"Yep," I said. I kissed her on the cheek, grabbed my skates, and climbed out of the car.

22

FINALLY

As expected, Yaz was on the ice, practicing jumps and spins. Watching her glide, I hoped she would actually make it to the Olympics someday or at least go to Nationals. Yaz Kilroy really is amazing. As soon as she saw me, she waved and zoomed toward me.

"Where've you been? I called your house on Saturday and Daisy told me you were gone for the weekend," Yaz said as she came off the ice, slid on her plastic blade guards, and joined me on the bleachers. Her smile revealed shiny new braces.

"You got braces!" I shrieked.

"Do I look ugly? Tell me the truth," she demanded.

Yaz was so extremely cute, she could never look ugly, and that's what I told her.

"You'd better not be lying, V," she warned, then questioned me again. "So where'd you go?" My friend Yaz not only badgers—like a detective, she asks a lot of questions.

"I went to an art exhibit in Seattle."

"Oh, I thought maybe you went somewhere exciting."

"It was my grandmother's art show and I got to meet her for the first time and on Saturday I'm going with her to Los Angeles for a week and to Disneyland, I hope," I rambled.

"Your black grandma?"

"Yep."

Yaz scrunched up her face and said, "That's weird."

"What's weird?" I asked.

"That you're eleven years old and you never met her. Where's she been?"

Right then, I was happy and I really didn't feel like talking about the embarrassing Roxanne Diamond story, so I just answered, "Living in another country."

Of course that wasn't enough of an answer for Yaz the interrogator. "Where?"

I blurted out, "Paris."

"Paris isn't a country, V. There's even a city called Paris in Texas."

I squinted at her out of the corner of my eye. "Paris, France, and Berlin and Africa, too."

That seemed to satisfy Yaz, and when they started to play music in the rink, she ordered me to put on my skates and dragged me off the bleachers. Onto the ice we sailed and did some ice dancing to the rhythm.

Later, when Yaz's mom, Mrs. Kilroy, showed up, Yaz blabbed to her about my grandma from Paris, France, and something in the way Mrs. Kilroy looked at me made me wonder if she knew the whole story. She and my mom do talk now and then.

But lucky for me, Mrs. Kilroy didn't give me away. She just smiled and said, "How nice that you *finally* got to meet her." It seemed like the only word I heard was *finally*.

23

SHOPPING

After dinner that night, Mom showed up at my door and said, "We're going shopping, V . . . c'mon."

"Shopping?" I love shopping. I grabbed my pack and off we went.

"Does Roxanne live in a house or an apartment?" I asked as we climbed in the car.

"A house. In an older, very charming, interesting neighborhood," Mom said as we pulled out of the driveway.

"Good interesting or bad interesting?" I asked. "Is Roxanne poor or something?"

"No, it's a very nice neighborhood, mostly black. It used to be the center of a lot of African American cultural life in Los Angeles. It's the house your father grew up in. It isn't modern like ours, but . . . she's hardly poor."

Remembering the price tags I'd seen on her artwork, I said, "I didn't think so, because her paintings sure cost a lot."

"But some artists only sell a few paintings a year," Mom explained.

"Then maybe we should buy one of her paintings," I suggested.

"Maybe we should."

"Just not that labyrinth mind one . . . it was scary."

Mom laughed and said, "I always looked forward to seeing his family's home, but it was never to be. He said he'd practically grown up in an art gallery. I'm glad you'll get to see it."

"Maybe you will, too, someday," I told her.

"Maybe," she replied.

At the mall, I got to pick out two dresses and a new bathing suit and a purple tank top with matching shorts. I love purple. Then we went to the shoe store and I got new sandals.

"Are you buying all this stuff for my trip? I'm only going to be gone for a week."

Mom took my hand. "I want it to be very special for you, V, that's all."

So do I.

24

AIRPORTS AND AIRPLANES

Though being in charge of a hotel seems like it would be fun, whenever I go to the airport, I begin to think working there would be okay, too, especially if I got to fly to a lot of different places. And when I say fly, I don't mean being a flight attendant, I mean being a pilot.

I knew there were female pilots because we'd taken some flights where a woman was the captain, and I'd been on others where black men were the pilots, but I'd never seen an African American female pilot.

"Are there black women who fly planes?"

"Of course," Mom replied. "Remember that book you read about the pilot Elizabeth Coleman?"

I did. "But that book was about almost a century ago.

I mean black women who fly planes now . . . and big planes that carry lots of people, not little airplanes like in that book."

"Oh, you mean commercial pilots."

"I suppose . . . I was thinking flying airplanes might be cool, and I was just wondering if they would let me become that or not."

Mom's face got the insect-sting look and she abruptly stopped walking, so I stopped with her. "They? Who's they?" she asked.

"The people in charge of stuff. I mean, for a long time they didn't let black people do certain jobs even though they were smart enough. Remember why Martin Luther King and his friends had to march to Washington and stuff? And it's a whole new century and all Yaz talks about is being the first African American female to win an Olympic ice skating gold medal. Mr. Kilroy says that after all these years she should at least be the second or maybe even the third. He says certain things are different if you're black."

"Certain things are different if you're black," she repeated, but it wasn't a question.

"Yep, like Yaz's mom is always telling her she has to work harder at ice skating because of her color. She's says there's still prejudice, but most people try to pretend there isn't. And I think maybe she's right, because sometimes people look at me and you funny, but mostly older people. So I don't want to try to be something if I'm going to have to work harder because I'm black."

"Violet Diamond, haven't I taught you that you can be anything you want to be? And I'm certain there are African American female commercial pilots. There have to be. You can research that on your computer when you get back home."

At that point, Mom took my hand and we started walking again toward the terminal.

"Or maybe I can look it up online when I'm with Roxanne. She has to have a computer, right?"

Again, Mom stopped walking, and this time she kind of yanked my hand. I felt like a dog on a leash. "I think you should call her a grandmother name instead of Roxanne. It doesn't sound very respectful."

"Hmm . . . I think I'll figure that out with her. I mean, I know I don't want to call her Gam, and Grandma doesn't really fit her. I'll let you know when I get back. Can we go now before I miss the plane?"

Roxanne Diamond was waiting at the security checkpoint. Unlike the greeting we got at the gallery, Roxanne rushed over, smiling. "I thought maybe you weren't coming."

"My mom wouldn't do that. When she makes a promise, she always keeps it," I proudly told her.

"That's good to know," Roxanne replied.

Before we got in the security line I hugged my mom tightly and I grabbed my carry-on case.

"I'll take good care of her," Roxanne promised my mom, patting her shoulder. They both had tears in their eyes.

Just as we got to the terminal, a last call to board for Los Angeles came over the loudspeaker. "That's our flight," Roxanne said.

I scurried toward the doors that led to the plane. "C'mon, Roxanne!" I yelled.

25

BIBI

Even though she was my grandmother, because I'd only met her twice before, it was like being with a stranger.

Sitting in the seat beside me, Roxanne kept staring at me.

When is this plane going to take off?

"I'm not trying to be impolite, but you're sort of making me feel like a zoo animal," I whispered.

"I'm sorry," she whispered back.

The engine began to roar and the pilot started talking and when the flight attendants gave their safety talk, I memorized the exits.

"Do you think it'd be fun to fly a plane?" I asked her.

"It's lots of fun, Violet," she replied.

"No way . . . you flew an airplane?"

"Yep. I took a few lessons in a two-seater plane a long time ago."

I studied her face to see if she was lying and decided she wasn't. "Wow. Did you get a pilot's license?"

"No, my uncle had been a Tuskegee Airman and he used to take me up with him when I'd go to visit him during the summer. So I suppose flying is in my blood."

"A real Tuskegee Airman, seriously?"

No wonder I like airplanes. It must be in my blood, too.

"So you know who they were?"

I nodded. "Of course, we learned about it in school. I even know about Elizabeth Coleman, the first black woman to get an international pilot's license, because I bought a book about her at the book fair."

"I see," she said.

"So is the Tuskegee Airman guy still alive?"

"Yep," she replied. This was the second time she'd said it. And I thought I was the only person who said *yep*.

"Do you think maybe he'll take us flying?"

"His flying days are long gone, Violet . . . He lives in Memphis with his daughter, and he's almost a hundred years old and in a wheelchair."

Right then, the plane started moving and soon we were ready for takeoff. Faster and faster it went until finally we were off the ground. "This is my favorite part," I told her.

"Mine too."

I gazed out the window at the city below, and soon we were soaring. I love soaring.

During the flight, I started the what-name-I-should-call-you conversation.

"Mom thinks I should call you a grandmother name instead of Roxanne," I confided.

"What do you think?" she asked me.

I shrugged. "Don't know. Did you know that Roxanne means 'star'?"

"Yep."

"Do you always say *yep*?"

She smiled and nodded.

"Because I do, too . . . anyway . . . back to what I should call you."

"I did a little digging and came up with the name Bibi. What do you think of that?" she replied.

"Bibi?" I'd never heard anyone call their grandma that before. "How do you spell it?"

"B-i-b-i. It's Swahili for 'grandmother,'" she replied.

"Swahili?" I'd done some research about Swahili, and this seemed like a good time to impress her. "There are only five countries where Swahili is the official language. TDUCK."

"TDUCK?" Roxanne repeated.

"Tanzania, Democratic Republic of the Congo, Uganda, the Comoros, and Kenya. TDUCK." The pleased look she gave me let me know I could instantly add her name to my *people who think Violet Diamond is incredibly smart* list.

"You're very smart, aren't you? Your dad was very smart."

The last time she'd talked about my dad, it had made her cry. Quickly, I made a silent prayer-wish that she wouldn't start boohooing, and when I glanced up at her face, her eyes were dry. *Whew.*

"So what do you think about calling me Bibi?" she asked.

"Bibi," I repeated. Just saying it made me smile. "I like it a lot."

And so Roxanne Kamaria Diamond became my bibi.

The landing was very un-smooth. The plane skidded and did a couple of hops in the air, and I held my breath. *Please let me live,* I thought. Finally, we came to a stop and I breathed.

"That was a really bad landing," I told Bibi as we gathered our things.

"Really bad."

"Don't worry, Bibi. I'll do a better job than that when I'm a pilot."

26

LOS ANGELES

There was one thing I had to do as soon as I got off the plane—buy postcards, because I'd promised Athena, Yaz, and Daisy. And if I didn't mail them by at least tomorrow, I'd probably be back home by the time they arrived, and that seemed silly.

"I have to buy postcards before we leave," I told Bibi. "Is that okay?"

"Of course, Violet," Bibi said as she reached in her purse and took out her wallet.

"It's okay, I have my own money," I told her, and when I made a beeline to one of the stores, Bibi was right behind me.

Before long, I'd picked out five postcards and a

refrigerator magnet. I held up the magnet of the Holly-wood sign for Bibi to see. "It's for my mom."

"I'm sure she'll like it."

We loaded onto the shuttle bus that was going to take us to the parking lot where she'd left her car, and on the way I noticed a building that looked like a flying sau-cer had landed in the middle of the airport. "What's that place?" I pointed. "It reminds me of the Space Needle."

"That's called the Theme Building. It was built in 1961, if I remember correctly. There's a restaurant inside."

"Can we go there now?" I pleaded.

"I think you need reservations, but I'll call and see," Bibi said, and reached for her cell phone.

Reservations? That spelled probably expensive. I remembered what Mom had said about some artists not making too much money and said, "Never mind."

But she was already talking on the phone, and who-ever was on the other end must have given her good news, because she got a big smile on her face and said, "The name is Roxanne Diamond. Thank you so much. Yes, fifteen minutes."

"Lucky us. There was a cancellation," Bibi told me, and the next thing I knew we were skedaddling off the bus. Towing our suitcases, we took the elevator up into the saucer.

I don't know about Bibi, but I felt pretty excited. Some

of the food on the menu was the usual fancy-schmancy restaurant stuff, but then I saw just what I felt like eating, an extra tasty spicy cheeseburger. And that's what I ordered, along with fries and a big glass of lemonade.

Bibi ordered a Cobb salad and mineral water, and for dessert we shared a chocolate lovin' spoon cake, which tasted so good, I wished we'd ordered two.

I watched her as she pulled out her purse to pay the bill and was glad that we look alike, that our skin is almost the same color, that her eyes are as brown as mine. There would be no question marks in people's eyes today.

And as we got up to leave, a smiling brown-skinned man, lady, and girl about my age came in and were led to their table. I heard the girl call the man "Daddy." The smiling man was holding his daughter's hand.

I wish my daddy was with us.

And he would kiss my forehead the way her daddy just did.

And look at me with love in his eyes.

"Can we go there again?" I asked as Bibi and I climbed back onto the shuttle bus.

"Los Angeles is a big place and there's lots to do, Violet," she replied.

"Like Disneyland?" *Please please please.*

"Like Disneyland."

"Tomorrow?"

She shook her head. "Tomorrow is Sunday."

"So?"

"Tomorrow we'll go to church and then we'll have the Diamond Family Sunday Feast," she informed me.

The way they always do when I get nervous, my insides got squiggly. "Huh? There's more family? But Mom told me there was only you."

"Same as my mother, I was an only child and what distant family I have left on her side is in New York City."

"New York City? Can we go there? I really want to go there bad. It's number one on my list of places I want to go to."

"Someday, Violet . . . but about Sunday dinner," Bibi explained, "I'm talking about your grandfather's family."

"But my grandfather's dead, isn't he?"

"Yes, he died years ago, but a few members of his family live in Los Angeles and we take turns hosting the Diamond Family Sunday Feast. Tomorrow's my turn to cook."

"Will other kids be coming?"

"Only one."

"My cousin?" I asked.

Bibi answered, "Yep."

"Awesome."

27

A STREET LINED
WITH PALM TREES

The street where Bibi lived was lined on both sides with palm trees so tall, it looked like they were trying to touch the blue sky. "Wow! It's pretty here."

Bibi smiled.

With one exception, all of the palm tree trunks leaned in the same direction. "Wonder why that one didn't grow the same as the others?" I asked.

"Same as some people . . . probably born different. Like me, I suppose. Everyone warned me not to pursue my art, said it was a waste of time. Colored girl, artist. Most folks laughed, even my daddy. Told me to be a social worker . . . even a nurse. But the art was in my mind and soul and it had to come out. I couldn't help it.

No matter what, it kept showing up." Bibi gazed up at the palm trees, then at me.

I thought for a few seconds about what she had said.

I felt different inside, too. "I think words are in me," I said. "Just when I think there are no more to learn, another one shows up."

"Maybe you'll be a writer."

"A writer? I never thought about that, but being a writer might be cool, very cool."

Bibi unlocked the gate and we entered the front court-yard of her house. Inside, there was a garden with all sorts of cacti, a bunch of other plants, and one patch along the wall with nothing but blooming yellow sunflowers.

"Sunflowers are my favorite," I told her.

"Mine too," she replied. "We'll pick some later, okay?"

"Sure."

The house was painted a color that was sort of red-orange and it had a red tiled roof and a big stained glass window. It looked like pictures I'd seen in books about Mexico. "Is this a Mexican house?" I asked.

"It's Spanish style. Quite a few of the houses in this section of Leimert Park are."

"Leimert Park? I thought this was Los Angeles?"

"It is Los Angeles . . . a part of South Los Angeles, but some neighborhoods have special names." Bibi put the key in the lock and led me inside. A bunch of mail from the door mailbox slot blocked the entryway floor, and she hurried to gather it up. "My house is a mess," she said. "Forgive me. I wasn't expecting company." Then she excused herself to go to the bathroom.

I stored my suitcase and backpack in a corner and headed to the living room, where I plopped on the sofa and looked around. It wasn't like any room I'd ever seen before and I loved it. The walls, including the ceiling, were painted lavender and the wood around the windows was painted the color of salmon. Every wall was covered with all sorts of paintings and other kinds of artwork. There were wooden statues and stuff made from clay crammed everywhere. One whole shelf had nothing but turquoise figurines, maybe thirty in all. There was enough art for a museum, and that was just in the living room. From what I could see from where I was sitting, the dining room's four walls, which were painted bright yellow, were covered with more paintings and face masks.

She needs a bigger house.

And that's exactly what Bibi said when she came out of the bathroom. "I need a bigger house, don't I, Violet?"

"Just call me V, okay? It's what most people call me. Even my mom, except when she's mad."

"V it is, then . . . but if I forget now and then, will you forgive me? I'm getting old."

"How old are you?"

"Old enough."

"That's what my gam always says when I ask her."

Bibi chuckled. "Smart woman."

She gave me a tour of the house. There was a small den, painted bright green, with a flat-screen TV, two recliner chairs that looked comfy, and a desk with a laptop computer. She showed me her bedroom, which was pretty messy, like my room at home. It was painted bright orange.

I thought about the walls in our house.

Boring.

"You sure like pretty colors," I commented.

The next bedroom was very neat and was painted bright blue. Periwinkle, Bibi called it. It had a fluffy bed. "This will be your room, Violet," Bibi said.

My own room here.

But the room across from it was a little dark because the drapes were closed. Inside, I could see there was no bed, just an old-looking dresser and an entire wall of framed papers and photographs. It was the only room in the house that was painted white. "Is it okay if I look at the pictures?"

Bibi nodded and flicked on the light.

From a distance, I thought I saw pictures of me, and as I got closer I realized I was right. My school photos were labeled for every year, beginning with kindergarten.

Her having my pictures there made me start to feel a little less like a guest.

Above mine were school pictures of my dad.

My mom had lots of photos of him from when they were married, but none from before. He was so cute. "Was this his room?" I asked.

Bibi picked at her nails and replied, "Yes, it was. Till the day he left for college. Once New York City bit him, he rarely came home except for Christmas. Summertime would come and he'd promise, but then he'd get a summer job or internship there."

I inspected the photos again. "We really look alike, huh?"

"Yes, you do."

Also on the wall were a bunch of his framed diplomas and awards. One said *class valedictorian.* "What's a valedictorian?"

"The highest-ranked student in the graduating class. He gave an amazing speech. We were the proudest parents who ever lived. I can still hear his voice. 'My name is Warren Thurgood Diamond and I was sent here to inspire you.'"

"His middle name was Thurgood . . . like Thurgood Marshall?"

That made Bibi smile. "Yep," she replied. "His father wanted him to be a lawyer, but from the time he was little, Warren had his mind set on being a surgeon."

I examined every corner of the room with my eyes. I wanted to be able to see him, hear his voice, talk to him.

I felt like he'd been stolen from me. "Do you think maybe his ghost is in here?"

Bibi gave me a you're-a-strange-person look and replied, "No. I think his spirit is with God."

"In heaven?" I asked.

"Of course."

I suppose because her eyes were getting watery again, she changed the subject. "Want to see my studio? It's outside."

I glanced at the photos one more time. Knowing they were here, where I could see them anytime, made me happy. I shut off the light and trailed Bibi outside to the backyard. About ten wind chimes and a hundred Christmas ornaments dangled from the patio. Some were stars and others were globes in every color. "Wow. Are these always here?"

"Always."

I felt as if I was in an odd, unique, and beautiful world. Like maybe we'd left the Earth.

"It's just a converted garage," she said as she turned the knob and welcomed me inside her studio.

Inside there were easels and canvasses, big and small. All around there were paints and cans, a zillion brushes, and the floor was so spattered with paint of every color that it looked like a painting itself. She even had one of those wheel things for making pottery. "I'm afraid it's not very organized," she apologized.

"That's okay, my gam's office isn't organized, either," I told her, then asked, "Do you sell a lot of paintings?"

"Enough to put some travel money in my pocket. I have a serious case of wanderlust."

A great new word. "Does that mean you like to wander around?"

"To travel," she explained.

I grinned. "I have that, too."

Bibi walked toward me, reached out, swallowed me up with her arms, and hugged me tight, and I hugged her back. Right then, Bibi seemed less like a stranger. She felt warm and smelled nice, like a vase of flowers.

I rummaged through the studio, looking at this and that, touching the paintings and containers of paint. "I don't think I have art inside me like you do because I'm not that good at drawing and I never really painted except in school art class, but I really want to learn. Can you teach me?"

"Yes, Violet, I will," she promised, "but right now Bibi needs to go inside and put her feet up. The old girl is getting tired. Later on we'll go to the market. I need some things for tomorrow's dinner." Like a tail on a donkey, I was right behind her.

"Are you hungry or thirsty?"

I rubbed my still very full tummy. "After that ginormous lunch, no way."

We went to the den and she turned on the TV with the

remote. "You mind the Cooking Channel?" she asked. "Might give us some ideas for tomorrow's dinner."

"Okay," I replied, then glanced at the computer. "But is it okay if I send my mom and Daisy an e-mail?" I asked.

"Of course." Bibi turned on the computer and logged on. "There you go, sweetie."

Sweetie?

I sent a short e-mail to my mom and Daisy, letting them know everything was okay, and in no time at all they replied with happy faces. "Done," I said, and turned off the laptop.

Bibi settled down in the recliner, put her feet up, and motioned for me to sit in the other chair. "Been a very long week," she sighed.

We watched the Cooking Channel for a while before Bibi nodded off and snored. Outside, the wind began to blow and an orchestra of chimes clanged.

I like it here.

But as she napped, I caught myself wondering if Bibi would sneak into my room at night and check on me, the way Gam does when I spend the night at her house. I hadn't even been gone a day, but I already missed my comfy bed, Mom, Daisy, Gam, and Poppy, the same everyday mostly boring stuff that goes on in Moon Lake, my kitty, Hazel, motormouth Athena, Yaz, shouting orders on the ice.

Violet Diamond is a little homesick.

28

A MILLION MILES
FROM HOME

About a half hour later, Bibi woke up and we headed to the market to buy food for tomorrow's dinner.

The grocery store wasn't too far from her house, and inside, almost everyone was African American. There were a few people who I knew were from Mexico or someplace like that because I heard them speaking Spanish, but I didn't see one single white person. It was nothing like Moon Lake, where I'm usually the only black person in the store, or even Seattle, where there are all kinds of people, and being in a place where nearly everyone was African American for the first time felt different. Even though I was still in America, it felt like I'd traveled a million miles from home.

"I'm in the mood for a soul food feast. What do you think, V?"

I shrugged. "I suppose."

"Ever had grits pie?" Bibi asked.

"I've had grits, but never in a pie. Doesn't sound delicious."

"Well, it's a family favorite, V. My grandmother from Louisiana used to make it. Thought you and I should give it a try. I know her recipe by heart . . . think the only thing I don't have at home is vanilla extract and buttermilk."

It was as if Bibi had memorized the store and she knew right where everything was.

"And for the lemon icebox pie . . . I'll need some condensed milk."

"That sounds good," I said as I tagged along beside her.

"It is and it's easy," Bibi told me.

Then, like she was writing a menu inside her head, she rattled off, "And short ribs, salmon croquettes, fried okra, jambalaya, and corn bread."

By the time we finished shopping, the cart was filled almost to the top, and it was almost dark when we loaded up the car and headed back to her house.

"You getting hungry, V?" she asked.

"You must be reading my mind," I told her.

"Taco Bell okay with you?"

I told her yes and in a flash she'd changed lanes. Minutes later we pulled into the drive-through and ordered.

I'm not sure why, but being with Bibi felt different from being with Gam. Not better, just different. It was like one was mint chip ice cream and the other was cookies 'n' cream: I like them both and both are sweet.

That night, I showered and washed my hair in Bibi's pretty bathroom that had black and yellow tiles. While my hair was still wet, she rubbed in something called Moroccan argan oil. It made my hair really easy to comb through, even easier than the stuff Yaz had helped me buy. Bibi said I could have the small bottle. She promised it would keep my hair soft and shiny but not greasy. "Thanks, Bibi."

And later, as I climbed into bed, she asked, "Do you say your prayers with your mother or by yourself?"

"Oh, I just make wishes, but Mom claims they're really prayers," I explained.

Bibi's face turned serious. "Do you believe in God, V?"

I answered yes and pointed up. "I know He's up there."

She kissed my forehead and said, "Good night and God bless."

29

THE SUNDAY MORNING PARTY

If being at the market had made me feel like I was in another country, church the next morning made me wonder if I was in a faraway galaxy.

It was called the Holy Trinity First Baptist Missionary Temple of Los Angeles. "Huh?" I asked.

"Mostly we just say Holy Trinity," Bibi whispered. She was wearing a white suit and matching white shoes, not African clothes. In fact, since we'd left Seattle, I'd never seen her in African clothes.

"How come you don't wear African clothes anymore?" I asked.

"I only wear African garb for art events . . . it feels right to present myself that way."

One person was warming up the organ, another the

piano, and a man strummed a guitar. The choir was just getting in place. We were early and the church was only about half full. "If you don't get here early, it's hard to get a seat," she explained.

Lots of people knew Bibi, and when one lady called her Sister Diamond, I asked, "Is she really your sister? I thought you didn't have any."

"We are Sisters in the Lord and interconnected by the Holy Spirit," she explained. "Church Sisters."

We hadn't been there very long before I found out that Bibi had a whole bunch of Sisters in the Lord.

With a proud look she introduced me over and over again as her granddaughter. "My . . . my . . . ain't you a pretty little thing," one of the women, who Bibi called Sister Williams, told me. She was wearing a bright blue suit with rhinestone buttons and a hat in the same color that had three peacock feathers.

"Thank you . . . I like your hat," I replied.

"Some of the women here sure dress pretty," I told Bibi. Bibi smiled.

By ten o'clock, Holy Trinity was packed with African American people, old and young and in between, and the church was filled with music and singing.

Suddenly, a man in a black suit appeared on the stage. "Welcome to the Sunday morning party! Hallelujah! Praise the Lord!" he shouted.

People all around me, including Bibi, stood up, raised

their arms, and shouted, "Praise Jesus!" Some were clapping their hands and moving with the music and others sang along with the choir. It almost felt like I was at a concert, so I stood up and clapped to the beat.

Then unexpectedly, everything got quiet. And as if they'd practiced it many times before, everyone began to sit down. It was like someone had let all of the air out of a balloon. Soon, I was the only one standing. Gently, Bibi took my hand and sat me down.

"Now what?" I asked.

"Shhh."

The guy up front wearing the black suit quietly said, "Good Sunday morning. What a pleasure it is to have each and every one of you here today."

All around me people answered, "Good Sunday morning."

And when he commanded the people to open their Bibles to a certain place, like robots, everyone who had a Bible did.

Bibi scooted me close to her and pointed with her finger to where everyone was reading and together we read along. It was in a section of the Bible called Proverbs.

Then, like a teacher, the guy up front started to talk about what we'd just read. Some people even took notes. I wondered if later there'd be a test.

During the rest of the service, the choir sang more songs and the preacher did a lot more teaching from the

Bible and everyone took a communion wafer and ate it, including me. I closed my eyes and waited to feel more holy, but I didn't. Maybe I would later. When I opened my eyes and gazed up at Bibi, she was grinning at me. And I grinned back.

30

THE DIAMOND FAMILY
SUNDAY FEAST

"Normally, I would stay at church and socialize for a while, but you and I have some serious cooking to do," Bibi said as we nearly sped back to her house.

"What time will they be here?" I asked.

"Six."

I glanced at the kitchen wall clock. It was just after noon.

Bibi hurried to change her clothes and advised me to do the same. "Around here the cooks get their clothes dirty."

First we diced onions, celery, green onions, bell peppers, tomatoes, and garlic, and set it aside. Then we got the short ribs going. Next we put on the butter beans. And after that we chopped up the chicken for the jambalaya.

Even with the kitchen door and window open, it was hot and both of us were sweating.

"Maybe we should turn on the air conditioner?"

Bibi laughed and pointed to the window. "You're looking at it," she replied.

The smells from the food filled the kitchen and Bibi was humming happily when she decided to put on a CD. "You like Nina Simone?"

Not knowing who Nina Simone was, I shrugged.

The music sounded like it was from a long time ago, but it was still good.

"She's my favorite . . . well, she and Nancy Wilson," Bibi said, and began singing along about Sunday in Savannah, swaying to the melody.

We were working fast, but I liked it and wondered if this was what it felt like to be a restaurant chef. In my mind, I added chef to my list of potential careers.

By four o'clock everything was cooked or still baking, and Bibi gave me a high five.

Together we put the extension in the dining room table and brought in chairs from the closet so there were enough seats for seven people. We each took an end of the white lace tablecloth and lifted it. Like a parachute it floated to the table. Bibi took out her real silverware from the china cabinet, good dishes, and cloth napkins, and we set the table.

"Do you always make it so deluxe?" I asked.

"Deluxe? That's a funny word for someone your age to use."

"I like funny words," I told her.

Bibi stopped what she was doing, clutched a gold-rimmed dish to her chest, and smiled at me. "You're so much like your father," she replied. "And to answer your question, no, I don't usually make it so deluxe, but this is a special occasion," she added.

"Because I'm here?"

"Yep . . . because you're here. Been a long time since I shared this house with anyone." For a few nanoseconds, she stared kindly into my eyes, then said we should get dressed.

I went to my room, slipped on my purple and lavender striped dress, and was gazing in the mirror, fixing my curls, when the doorbell rang.

Right away, loud voices came from the living room, a man's deep one and a boy's voice.

I stepped out of the bedroom and heard the boy yell, "So where is she?" He zoomed into the hallway, and as soon as he saw me he ran toward me so fast, we bumped into each other and I nearly fell.

"You should really watch where you're going," I told him.

"Mr. Diamond!" the man shouted from the other room. "What'd I tell you about running in the house?"

"Mr. Diamond" was just my height, with brown skin, dark eyes so big they looked like any minute they might pop out of their sockets, and a round face. Something about him reminded me of a grasshopper. I tried not to, but I couldn't stop myself and I giggled.

He sneered. "What's funny?"

"Nothing," I said, then asked, "What's your name?"

It sounded like he said, "I'm Ed."

"Hi, Ed," I replied.

"Not Ed." He snickered and spelled out A-M-H-E-D. "Amhed. It means 'highly praised.'"

Right then I felt like what Poppy calls a nincompoop. "Oh."

The man came up behind Ahmed. "Violet?" he asked.

"Why're you askin' her that? You can tell it's her from those pictures on the wall," Ahmed told him, and stared at me hard. "She looks just like those pictures, doesn't she?"

The man was tall, about as brown as me, and bald, with freckles on his cheeks. "Nice to meet you. I'm your second cousin Harris." He reached out to shake my hand.

"Hi, I'm Violet," I told him.

"We already know that," Ahmed teased.

"And this is my son, Ahmed."

"Hey," Ahmed said.

"Hi," I replied.

The way these two were gawking at me, I felt like a mannequin in a store window. And I was glad when the doorbell rang again.

As if it were his house, Ahmed shouted, "I'll get it!" and bolted to the living room.

Harris and I stopped at the kitchen, where Bibi was still working on dinner.

"Smells awful good in there," he told her, then turned to me. "Your grandma's a mighty good cook. You could learn a little something from her."

I beamed. "I helped Bibi with the whole feast."

"Bibi? Who's Bibi?" he asked.

"I'm Bibi. It's Swahili for 'grandmother,'" she informed him.

"Lord have mercy! Here you go with that Africa mess again. This is not Africa, Roxanne. Let the child call you Grandma."

Bibi turned up her nose at him and went back to cooking. "As usual, Harris, I'm ignoring you. And this is not your business."

"I like Bibi," I told him. "Really."

"All right then. So what'd you cook for us, *Bibi*?" Harris started looking in the pots.

"I know you'd better get outta my kitchen before I hurt you. And where's your wife?"

"Victoria had to work a few extra hours at the hospital. One of the other nurses had some kind of emergency. She'll be here after while."

Harris grabbed one of the hot hush puppies Bibi had

just taken out of the fryer, popped it in his mouth, grinned, and ducked out of the kitchen.

Whoever had rung the bell had come inside, and I heard women's voices in the living room. I peeked in and saw two ladies who were dressed the same except for their shoes and looked just alike. Twins. Their faces looked older than my mom's, who is in her forties, but younger than Bibi's, who's *old enough*.

"Roxanne Diamond! Do I smell short ribs?" the one wearing red shoes asked as she made her way to the kitchen.

As soon as Bibi saw her, she stopped what she was doing, dried her hands on her apron, and hugged her for a long time. The two of them were still hugging when the woman finally noticed me and pushed Bibi away. "This your grandbaby?" she shrieked. And then whoever she was hugged me—hard. "I'm your cousin Lorna Diamond. We've waited a lot of years to meet you."

"I'm Violet."

She turned to Bibi. "And she's beautiful, too! And look at all that hair." She glanced my way and asked, "That is your real hair, isn't it?"

"Yep, it is."

"Hard to tell now'days," Lorna told Bibi.

With all that commotion, the other woman, whose shoes were yellow, had come into the kitchen. "Hi, I'm Violet," I told her, and stuck out my hand for her to shake.

But that didn't stop her from hugging me just as tight as her twin sister had. "I'm Laura Diamond, Lorna's twin."

Obvious.

"Ain't she pretty, Laura?" Lorna asked.

"As a picture," Laura replied.

Later, I would find out that Lorna and Laura Diamond were both third-grade teachers. Neither had ever been married. The way they acted, it was kind of like they were married to each other. I wondered what it felt like to have an identical twin. Two Violet Diamonds—nope, I didn't want another me.

The last person to show up was Victoria, who rushed in uttering an apology. "Sorry to be late. Tell me y'all didn't eat yet." She was wearing pink nursing scrubs and her braided hair was pulled back into a ponytail. She smiled when she saw me.

"You must be Violet."

"Duh," Ahmed said.

"I'm your cousin-in-law, Victoria," she said, gave me a shoulder hug, and hurried to the bathroom to wash up.

Cousin-in-law? I didn't know there was such a thing.

Bibi, Lorna, and Laura began putting the food out on the buffet table, and I was just standing around. "Do you need me to help, Bibi?" I offered.

"Bibi?" the twins said at the same time.

"Swahili word for 'grandmother,'" Harris informed

them from where he was sitting in the living room, watching Poppy's favorite station, the Golf Channel.

"Bibi," Lorna and Laura repeated. "Cute," they added.

But Ahmed scowled. "Bibi? Why don't you just call her Grandma or Nana like I used to call my grandma before she died?"

For some reason, probably because everyone was fawning over me, treating me like I'm special, I was beginning to feel like a star. I looked Ahmed square in the face, cocked my head to the side, and replied, "I don't want to call her Grandma or Nana . . . I wanna call her Bibi."

Ahmed gave me a snide look. "Doesn't make any difference to me. You can call *my* auntie whatever you want."

My auntie? The way he'd said it made it sound like he owned her.

Creature.

"Time to eat!" Lorna shouted.

In a flash, everyone surrounded the table and joined hands while Bibi recited a short prayer. "Our Father in Heaven, we give thanks for the pleasure of gathering together for this occasion. We give thanks for this food prepared by loving hands. We give thanks for life, the freedom to enjoy it all, and all other blessings. Amen."

And all of the Diamonds, including me, echoed, "Amen."

The feast of foods-I'd-never-eaten-before was yummy.

And talk around the dinner table was filled up with jokes, stories, and a lot of laughing. None of them acted like they'd just met me—they treated me like they'd always known me. I liked this funny family and the way they made me feel—like I belonged to them.

31

EAVESDROPPING AGAIN

After dinner, because Bibi had cooked and Victoria had just gotten off work, Lorna and Laura stayed inside to clean up and made everyone else vamoose. Harris, Ahmed, Victoria, Bibi, and I were sitting on the back patio under the lit-up pergola when I excused myself to get some water.

"Other than that hair, you think she looks half white?" I heard either Lorna or Laura ask.

I stopped dead in my tracks and was getting ready to turn around and sneak back outside before they saw me, but when I thought about the truth I'd learned from eavesdropping on Mom and Gam a few weeks ago, I decided to stay out of sight and hear what else they had to say.

"If I didn't know you better, I'd accuse you of having

just made a very ignorant statement. What is half white supposed to look like, Halle Berry or Alicia Keys? There are many ways to look half white. Some of my biracial students have looked more white, others more black. Most of them have been somewhere in the middle. I had one girl who looked Persian. Biracial comes in just about every shade of skin, and all colors and kinds of hair, from pin straight to nappy. You can never predict what's going to come out of the mixed pot," the other answered.

"I know you're right," the other twin agreed. "I had a boy in my class who everyone thought was Latino until his black Jamaican daddy showed up on parent-teacher night."

"She's a pretty thing, isn't she? With that creamy brown complexion."

"And so intelligent, just like Warren. It's a shame he died so young."

"A shame," the other twin commented, and added, "I'll never forget his hundred-watt smile that could light up a room."

"Wasn't he always just as pleasant as could be?"

"As could be," she answered.

"And from the time he could read, always had his nose in a book. Lord, Roxanne sure loved that child."

"His dying broke her."

"It did," the other twin agreed.

What does that mean? I wondered.

"You think she looks half white?" one twin asked again.

"I suppose when you consider how dark brown her daddy was . . ."

"I know you'd better hush," her sister replied.

At that point I tiptoed to the bathroom, switched on the light, and closed the door. I got close to the mirror and stared at my reflection. Shy, shrinking Violet reappeared.

To white people, I'm half black.

To black people, I'm half white.

50% black + 50% white = 100% Violet?

Is that what I am, a percentage?

32

A DAY AT DISNEYLAND

Somehow, Ahmed got himself invited to Disneyland. If anyone had asked me, I definitely would have said no, but no one did. Bibi thought it was a good idea because he could go on the rides with me.

But as soon as we walked through the gates and into Disneyland, I didn't care anymore. It really was a Magic Kingdom.

"*My* auntie Roxanne takes me lots of special places whenever she's in town. And she brings me stuff back from places she travels to all the time."

"Good for you."

Creature.

For a few minutes or so, Ahmed shushed up. And then, the creature spoke as we strolled down Main Street

U.S.A. with Bibi trailing us. "One thing I wanna ask you. How come you got a *white girl* name instead of a *black girl* name?"

"You are so stupid. People can be named whatever they want."

"That so? I ain't never met no black girl named Violet."

"Have you met every black girl in the world?" I asked.

"Naw," he answered.

"So there. Plus, I'm not just black, in case you didn't know."

"But you look black."

"On the outside maybe, but inside my DNA, I'm white, too."

That seemed to shut him up for a while. Just a while.

"That place where you stay, it's mostly white, huh?"

"Moon Lake? Mostly."

Ahmed smirked. "What kinda joke name is that for a city, Moon Lake? You from outer space or somethin'?"

Why do I have to be with this annoying person all day long?

Lucky for me, Bibi must have heard him, because she yanked him by his collar and whispered something in his ear. I don't know what she said to him, but he got quiet.

Bibi took my hand, and with Ahmed beside us, we headed to Fantasyland.

We stayed at Disneyland until the nighttime fireworks show. My eyes were on the explosions of colored light in the sky when Ahmed asked Bibi, "Auntie Roxanne, remember that time you took me clear to New York City, just me and you?"

"Yep," she replied.

Ahmed turned to me and sneered. "We sure had a whole buncha fun, huh? Just me and you," he repeated.

Bibi grinned. "Yep, Ahmed. We sure did."

New York City, hmm? How many other trips have I missed out on?

On the drive back to Los Angeles, Bibi seemed tired.

"Thank you for taking me to Disneyland, Bibi. I always wanted to go there," I told her after we'd dropped off Ahmed and were finally alone.

"You're welcome, pickle."

"Pickle?"

"I'm sorry . . . it's what I used to call your daddy when he was little."

"Why'd you call him that?"

"That boy loved him some pickles, sour ones, sweet ones . . . didn't matter."

"Guess what? So do I," I told her.

Bibi grinned from ear to ear.

You would have figured that after all of that walking around Disneyland, I would have been so tired that as soon as I climbed into bed I would have conked off to sleep, but I didn't. Instead, I thought about Bibi and how I liked it best when it was just the two of us, like when we were cooking and listening to Nina Simone records.

Gam and Poppy I had to share, not only with Daisy but with their other grandchildren and my mom and my mom's sister and brother.

I'd just opened up a book to read when a gentle knock on my door cracked it open. "Are you asleep?" Bibi asked.

"Nope," I replied.

"Thought I'd give you a kiss good night and tuck you in. You're not too old for that, are you?"

I sat up in bed. "Not."

Even though Daisy claimed Bibi as her grandmother, too, and Ahmed seemed to want to own her as well, right then Bibi was all mine. And about that—I was glad.

33

HOLLYWOOD

The next morning, Bibi and I both slept in. "Gonna be a hot one," she said as we lounged on the back patio, her drinking coffee with cream, me chomping Cheerios. "So what's on our agenda today, V?" Bibi looked tired, and dark circles that looked like half-moons hung under her eyes.

"We could just hang out here, if you want, and you could teach me how to paint."

"Didn't you want to go to Hollywood?"

"I did, but we don't have to if you're tired," I told her.

"How about painting tomorrow? I have a hankering to take you to Hollywood today . . . can't come to Los Angeles without going to Hollywood."

I made a wish, then asked, "Is Ahmed coming with us?"

"No," Bibi replied.

Good.

I got dressed in a hurry, but Bibi was a slowpoke, and when I passed her room, she was sitting at her vanity, staring at her reflection, tying a scarf around her dreadlocks. In her bathroom, the shower was turned on, sending steam through the half-open door.

"Can I come in?" I asked.

She smiled. "Of course, Violet."

Beside the vanity was a tall jewelry box with six drawers, one of which was open. "Can I look?" I asked.

Bibi nodded. "It's mostly inexpensive. Trinkets from my travels. If you see something you like, it's yours."

She swept my hair back, fingered one of my pierced earlobes, and asked, "Why don't you pick out some earrings? I have some very pretty studs." She picked out a green pair. "You have a beautiful complexion. These emeralds would look good on you."

"I barely wear earrings. My ears are way too big. Plus, the way I wear my hair, no one would see them."

"You have lovely ears, Violet. Besides, in some cultures, large ears are prized possessions. Pick out anything you want," she replied, and headed to the bathroom.

"Even the emeralds?"

"Even the emeralds," she replied. "Just a quick shower," Bibi said as she entered the fogged-up room and closed the door.

I was betting she had all kinds of cool, interesting stuff, and I was right. Rings, old wind-up watches, a ton of earrings—some with no mates—brooches, bracelets, and chains. You name it. I opened one drawer, then another, trying on pair after pair of earrings, slipping rings on and off my fingers. Stuck in the side of one of the pillowed drawers, something caught my eye. It looked like a ring. I tried digging it out with my baby finger but couldn't, so I took a bobby pin from Bibi's dresser and finally pried it out. It was a gold ring, and I held it to the window, studying it closely, wondering if the stones, which looked like diamonds, were real or fake. There were supposed to be three stones, but the one in the middle was gone. I put the ring on my finger and admired the jewels as they glistened in the light.

Seconds later, when Bibi came out of the bathroom, I asked her, "Are these real diamonds? They kind of look like it. I did a report on diamonds this year." I held up the ring for her to see.

Bibi's eyes got big. "Where did you find it? I looked for it everywhere."

"It was stuck down in the side of one of the drawers and I had to dig it out." I slid the ring off my finger and gave it to her. "Are they real diamonds?"

"Yes, they're real," she answered as she clasped the ring with both hands and sat down on the foot of the bed. She had a strange look on her face.

"What's wrong?"

"Nothing's wrong. I thought it was gone forever." Bibi had tears in her eyes.

I plopped beside her. "Was it a present from your husband?"

"No, your daddy gave it to me one Mother's Day. Told me the three diamonds represented him, his father, and me. Get it, the three Diamonds."

"But one is gone."

"Fell out years ago, not long after your father died. I took it off one day, promising myself I was going to fix it, but then I never could find it." Bibi wrapped an arm around my shoulder. "Thank you."

I grinned big. "You're welcome . . . can we go to Hollywood now?"

We were lucky enough to find parking near Hollywood and Vine and strolled the Walk of Fame to Grauman's Chinese Theatre. I took lots of photos with my digital camera, and Bibi had hers, too. Over and over she asked people to take pictures of the two of us, and in every single one we were both smiling and happy.

"Y'all sure look alike," one lady who took our picture commented.

Bibi's face lit up like a lightbulb. "She's my granddaughter. Isn't she beautiful?"

Beautiful, me?

Bibi squeezed my hand.

In Madame Tussauds Wax Museum, where the replicas of people looked too real, Bibi took pictures of me with the wax figures.

"Freaky, huh?" I asked.

"Lifelike," she replied.

"Did you ever do sculptures of people?" I asked.

"I haven't for a very long time."

"Could you do one of me, please?" I begged.

"How about a painting? I'm better at that," she offered.

"A painting would be okay, too. Thanks."

From the wax museum we headed to the Hard Rock Cafe for lunch and afterward went to the Babylon Courtyard at Hollywood and Highland and took the escalators up to the viewing bridge to check out the Hollywood sign.

"Take a picture of me with the sign in the background, Bibi. I promised Daisy." I put on my sunglasses and posed. *Snap.*

Through a coin-operated telescope, I got a really close look at the Hollywood sign.

"What's it like to be famous?" I asked her as I gazed through the lens.

"I'm only famous in the art world, Violet. It's not the same as being a movie star," she explained.

"Oh. What's your favorite movie?" I asked.

"Dunno. Have a long list of favorites."

"C'mon, pick one."

Bibi gazed away into the sky. "*Lilies of the Field,* with Sidney Poitier," she answered.

"I never heard of that. What's it about?" I asked.

"A very good man. A man as good as your grandfather was."

My grandfather. I'd seen his pictures, but I knew almost nothing about him. "What was his name?"

"Moses. Moses Diamond."

"What kind of job did he have?"

"Got his degree from Prairie View College in electrical engineering, but back then, he couldn't find work as an engineer, so he set up his own business as an electrician," she told me.

"Where's Prairie View College?" I asked her.

"It's an African American college in Texas," Bibi replied.

"*Lilies of the Field* . . . can we rent that movie?"

Bibi smiled. "Sure thing, little sweet."

Little sweet?

Later, on the way home, as we sat in bumper-to-bumper traffic, Bibi proclaimed that taking La Brea Avenue at that time of day was a big mistake. "I should have known better."

I didn't care. I'd had a bunch of fun in my life, but this was one of the best times ever!

34

THE MISSING DIAMOND

The next day, we had a lazy morning, but in the afternoon we headed to a section of Downtown Los Angeles Bibi called the Jewelry District. Shop after shop window displayed bracelets, necklaces, rings, and other sparkly things. "Are we here to fix the ring?" I asked as we went into one of the stores.

Bibi held out her hand and flashed the ring. "Yes, indeed, time to replace that stone."

"Diamonds are expensive, huh?" I asked as I scanned the store jewelry cases.

"Yes, they're precious."

"You can find them in two kinds of volcanic rocks, and the word *diamond* comes from a Greek word, *adamas*.

There's no mineral on Earth that's harder, and they even use them to cut other jewels."

Bibi patted my cheek softly as a feather. "My, the things you know!"

"Can I help you?" a man asked Bibi from behind the counter.

"Yes," she replied, then took off her ring and held it out for the man to see. "One of the diamonds is missing. Can you replace it?"

The man studied the ring, and when he and Bibi started to talk, I asked if I could look around. "Yes, but stay inside the store, V."

I went from case to case in the huge store, imagining I owned all the pretty things, occasionally glancing over at Bibi. She and the man were having a long conversation.

After what felt like an hour, I watched as she paid the man with her credit card. "C'mon, Violet, let's go," she said.

"Did you get it fixed already?" I asked.

Bibi held her hand up for me to see and we both admired it. All three diamonds glistened, but even though Bibi was smiling, tears made water wells inside her eyes.

"What's wrong?" I asked.

"Nothing's wrong . . . nothing at all." Bibi embraced me and stroked my hair. "My Diamond's not missing anymore."

I didn't have to ask what she meant. I knew she was

talking about me. Her hug was long and made me feel like I was important in her life.

"I love you," Bibi whispered.

What should I say?

Should I tell her I love her, too?

I like her and she's nice, but . . .

"Thank you," I replied.

On the way home, we stopped at a bakery. Fancy cakes filled the display. "Which one do you want, Violet?" Bibi asked.

"Any one?" I eyed the cakes. "Red velvet with cream cheese frosting."

"We'll take it. And can you write 'Happy Birthday Violet' on it?" she asked the woman behind the counter. "And do you have candles?"

I tugged her sleeve. "It's not my birthday, Bibi," I said quietly.

"For every birthday I missed," she replied. Love shone from her.

And that night, after we'd eaten chili dogs with pickles and shredded cheese, Bibi brought out the cake, lit eleven candles, and sang the birthday song. The diamond ring on her finger caught the light and glimmered.

35

THE MASHED POTATOES

Since I'd gotten to Los Angeles, I'd mailed the post-cards and been sending Mom and Daisy daily e-mails, but that night, because I'd started missing them, I asked if I could call. Bibi said, "Of course."

"I went to the Hollywood sign," I bragged to Daisy.

"The Hollywood sign? You brat," she said playfully.

In the background, I heard Wyatt yell, *"Viva la Hollyweird!"*

He is so strangely odd!

"Can I talk to Mom?" I asked.

"Hey, Mom! The world traveler's on the line! Pick up, please!" D hollered.

"Hello, V." The sound of Mom's voice was better than dessert.

"Hi, Mom," I replied, and rattled off the events of the day.

"Sounds like you're having a great time."

"I am . . . and I met some of my dad's cousins, and Bibi's Sisters in the Lord at church—"

Mom interrupted, "Bibi? Who's Bibi?"

"Oh yeah, I forgot to tell you. Bibi is what I call Roxanne. It means 'grandmother' in Swahili. I like it, don't you?"

"Yes, I like it." I pictured the smile I knew was on Mom's face.

"And like I told you yesterday," I rattled on, "Disneyland was fun except for Ahmed, plus I've been taking lots of pictures . . . Is Hazel okay?"

Mom giggled. "Hazel is fine."

"Thanks for taking care of her for me."

"You're welcome, sweetie pie. What do you two have planned for tomorrow?" Mom asked.

"Bibi is going to teach me how to paint, but I don't think it's something I can learn in just a day . . . Are Gam and Poppy okay, too?"

"They miss you."

I asked to talk to them, but Mom told me they'd gone to the movies.

"Well, make sure they know I'll be home on Saturday. Are you all coming to the airport like you said?" I asked.

"Yes, and D's been nagging me to go to Serious Pie, so we're going there afterward."

"Cool and awesome . . . and one last thing. Bibi is flying back to Seattle with me because she wants to keep me company. She already bought her ticket. I just wanted you to know. Do you think she can go to Serious Pie with us?"

"Fine by me," Mom replied.

"Okay. See you on Saturday. Bye."

"I love you, V."

"Love you, too . . . Bye."

I hung up the phone and headed down the hallway to the kitchen, where Bibi was cooking dinner. "I told my mom that you're flying back with me and we're all going to Serious Pie!" I yelled out excitedly, and when I turned the corner to the kitchen, the mixer bowl filled with mashed potatoes was spinning like a merry-go-round.

"Sounds like a plan, V."

When she turned off the mixer, I stuck my finger inside, scooped up a taste, and put it in my mouth. "Yummy . . . What else are we having?"

"I have a pork loin on the grill. You like pork?"

"Yep, but what's a loin?"

"Long piece of pork that can be cut into steaks. I marinated it last night . . . And there's a salad that's waiting on you to put it together." Bibi pointed with her chin toward the counter. "I'm sure you know how to slice tomatoes and avocados. The lettuce is already washed."

I washed my hands and rolled up my sleeves. "Do you

have any red onion? Because red onion tastes good with avocado and tomato."

"I'm sure I do. Check the vegetable bin."

I rummaged through the bin and finally found one. *"Voilà,"* I proclaimed like a magician.

Bibi went outside to get the loin, and when she came back in, I was busy on the salad. "You're quite a little cook, aren't you?" she commented as she sliced the pork.

"I'm learning. A few weeks ago, Athena's gramma taught us how to make meat and macaroni pie. I could teach you, but it takes, like, all day."

"Who's Athena?"

"My best friend. She's Greek. Her gramma is staying with them because her mom just had a new baby. Mrs. Matsoukis, that's Athena's gramma, says we're all one human race . . . just in different colors."

Bibi stopped slicing and shook her head.

"What's the matter?"

"It's not so simple, Violet. White folks made the race laws in the first place, and our history is complicated."

"Oh . . . well, she lives in Greece, so she can't change any American laws."

"Your friend's grandmother is right . . . in a perfect world, we are all flesh and blood, the same species, one race, the human race. But this isn't a perfect world and most people insist on holding on to the many-race concept. I want you to be realistic, Violet. At this moment in time, on this planet Earth, in the eyes of most, even though you have a white mother, you are considered to be black. Do you understand me?"

"Yep, I really do. But if that's what you think, that we're all one race, why didn't you want my dad and mom to get married?"

"I don't feel that way anymore. In the past years, I've learned a lot. Now I realize, who am I to tell God who to join as one? Who am I to tell another person whom to love? My evolution was beginning right before you were born."

"I know. Mom told me about the letter you wrote but never got mailed."

Bibi glanced in my direction. "Did she tell you everything?"

"There's more?"

Bibi stopped cooking and sat down. "You're probably too young to understand."

I shrugged.

"After your father died, I got sick."

"Were you in the hospital?"

"Yes, a special hospital for people whose minds are broken. I was very depressed. I was in and out of that hospital several times. Then I ran away, traveled the world to try and forget."

"To forget my dad?" I asked.

"To forget the hurt."

"You seem okay now."

"I'm better. Time has been kind." Bibi hung her head. "I'm sorry, Violet. I was selfish, only thinking of myself, pretending you were better off without me. I told myself you didn't need me. There were many times I wanted to see you, call you, and there were days I promised myself to but didn't. I had myself convinced you had a nice life up there in Washington. You do, don't you?"

I nodded.

"I know you're still a child, so I don't expect you to understand all of this, but sometimes people make a mistake for so long that it starts to feel like it's not a mistake at all. And then one day, you tell yourself it's for the best." Bibi patted my arm. "Life had given me some roadblocks, but losing your father was my Waterloo."

"What's that mean?"

"My defeat."

Except for the sound of a siren in the distance, there was silence.

"In my nightly prayers, you were always at the top of my list. Always. I'm not perfect, Violet. Nowhere near perfect. Can you forgive me?"

"Yes," I replied.

Bibi pulled me to her, hugging me tight, and I hugged her back. The hug felt like love—love as good as Gam's and Poppy's. And afterward I felt so filled up with love, it was as if it was about to burst out of the top of my skull.

Right then, it seemed like a good time to change the

subject to something happy, so I did. "Do you have a secret ingredient for your mashed potatoes? Most old people have secret ingredients in their recipes."

"So I'm old people?"

"I'm sorry. I didn't mean . . ."

She smiled without showing her teeth and I could see a twinkle in her eyes. "You can't un-ring a bell, Violet."

I figured that one out fast. "Once it's done, you can't undo it, right?"

"Right. As for the mashed potatoes, I like to sneak in a little garlic and a pinch of fresh rosemary . . . gives it some zing."

"Thanks. Mashed potatoes are one of my favorite things."

"Mine too," she commented, then added, "Did you know they used to have a dance called the Mashed Potatoes?"

"Seriously?"

"Yep, and a song to go with it. I think I still have that record in my stack of forty-fives."

"What's a forty-five?"

"A forty-five RPM. One record, two songs . . . an A side and a B side."

"Can we listen to it?"

Bibi bolted from the kitchen to the living room and I followed. She pulled open a cabinet and slid out a shelf that had a bunch of black discs.

"Wow, old records? Can I see?"

"Sure. But be careful. Some of them are almost as old as me," she said with a wink.

"I found it!" I shouted. "'Mashed Potato Time' by Dee Dee Sharp." I flipped the record over. "And the B side is a song called 'Set My Heart at Ease.'"

She snapped a yellow plastic thing into the center of the record.

As if she was reading my mind, Bibi said, "It's called a spider."

Soon, the record was spinning and music filled the room.

"Show me the dance," I begged. "Is it hard?"

"No . . . it's so easy, almost anyone could do it." Bibi slipped off her shoes, got a little up on her toes, and, keeping time with the music, started mashing and turning her feet like someone trying to smash a bug over and over. She took me by the hands and in no time I was doing the Mashed Potatoes. When the record ended, we played it again. Bibi was smiling so big that her gums showed. I wondered if mine were showing, too.

After dinner, we sat in the living room, playing her favorite 78 RPMs, which were bigger than 45s and had a lot of songs, like a CD does. Nat King Cole, Nina Simone, Duke Ellington, Billie Holiday, and Nancy Wilson.

"Now, this is music," Bibi told me as the sun set.

Maybe, like Bibi's mashed potatoes, life has special ingredients, too—times that make it more special—stuff that gives it more zing. I closed my eyes and stored this time with her in my memory. And later, I promised myself, I'd start a new list. A list of times I will always remember.

36

THE BLUES

"What's gesso?" I asked as I examined a large plastic container in Bibi's studio. She was dressed in paint-stained jeans and an old yellow T-shirt that had the words *Peace, Love, and Happiness* plastered across the front.

"Surface prep for canvasses and other things people paint on. Goes on before you paint to seal the canvas and make it smooth."

I read the label. "Says you have to wait twenty-four hours minimum before you paint." I sure didn't want to wait a whole day before getting started. "Do we really have to put this stuff on first?"

Bibi pulled two large canvasses out from a shelf. "I

primed these a while back. I try to always have some ready for when the mood to paint strikes me."

"Do you only paint when the mood strikes you?"

"Not if there's a project I need to finish. Then it's the same as a"—she spelled out the word—"J-O-B."

"Is today a J-O-B, or did the mood strike you?"

"Neither. Today is a teaching day. Haven't done that in a while," she replied as she set up the matching blank white canvasses on side-by-side easels. "What's your favorite color, V?"

That wasn't an easy question to answer. "I think blue. Or maybe purple. I don't know."

"Ask yourself this question. What is the one color that always makes me feel good inside? Be decisive."

I took a few seconds before I blurted, "Okay, I choose blue."

"They're my favorites, too. There are about fifty-nine different colors of blue."

"Fifty-nine! That's a bunch."

Bibi pulled out a chart with different shades of blues and I studied the names. There was electric blue, Bleu de France, midnight blue, cobalt blue, Persian blue. "There are too many to memorize," I decided. I'd have to write them in my journal.

"For real," Bibi replied, and motioned for me to follow her to a wall that was lined with drawers. She opened one and I peered inside. Tubes and jars of paints were inside, all blues. "Pick one . . . the one that speaks to you."

I wanted to tell her that paints don't speak, but I knew what she meant. Finally, I fished out the one that I liked the best. "This one . . . ultramarine."

"Now for the palettes. We'll need large ones for this exercise," she said as she retrieved two.

"And brushes," I reminded her.

"Nope, no brushes. We'll use our fingers."

Finger painting? She'd better be kidding.

"I'm not a baby."

"It's just an exercise in color, Violet. There are all kinds of things to paint with: palette knives, rollers, fingers, not just brushes."

"I don't want to exercise. I just want to learn to paint with a brush . . . please, please, please and thank you very much."

The disappointment in my eyes must have shown, because she replied, "All right already, V. We'll use brushes, then."

"I want to paint a bird. Can you teach me to paint a bird? A blue bird."

Bibi let out the longest sigh I'd ever heard. "Yes," she replied, and asked, "A bird alone on the canvas?"

"No, in a tree. A pomegranate tree, because the fruit reminds me of red ornaments. And so I'm going to need some red and green, and I'm gonna name it *Blue Bird in a Pomegranate Tree on a Sunny Day.* So I'll need yellow for the sun."

Bibi chuckled. "Your persistence shouldn't surprise me. Warren was the same . . . once he made a decision, that was that. Sounds like you have your mind made up, Violet."

"Yep."

"We should at least sketch first, then." Bibi smiled and said, "First we'll sketch?"

From the way she pulled out the sketch pad, I could tell there was no getting around the sketch part.

Persistence definitely runs in the family.

"Do all artists sketch first?"

"Some sketch directly on the canvas, but I'm methodical."

"What's that mean?"

"I have a special method. First I sketch, sometimes in color, sometimes in black and white. Then, I sketch on the canvas. Then, I paint."

"Sounds like a lot of steps."

"I have to be careful for it not to consume me."

"I know what that means . . . like it eats you up."

"Yep, it eats me up so much that there are times I actually forget to eat. It's not healthy."

By the time we finished the sketch, Bibi had taught me about perspective, which made a lot of sense. And I suppose because she didn't want to be consumed, she declared it was time for lunch. "I could go for some fish. Does that sound good to you?"

I nodded and we headed to the car.

"Do all artists have to know this stuff about perspective and shading and fifty-nine different blues?"

"Most artists."

"I don't want to be an artist. I just want to do it for fun. It's supposed to be fun, right?"

"For some people it's a J-O-B, Violet. Remember that."

The fish place was called Fish Fry City and the neon sign outside said *You Buy We Fry.*

"What kind of fish would you like?" Bibi asked.

I studied the sign. "Do they have salmon?"

For some reason that made Bibi grin. "I don't think so," she replied.

"What are you gonna have?"

"My favorite, the catfish."

"Is it good?"

She licked her lips. "Delicious."

We both ordered the catfish, potato salad, and fruit punch. And minutes later, sitting on one of the outdoor tables with our food, I chomped away and thought, *Boy, was she right.*

On the way back to Bibi's house, her cell rang in the car's Bluetooth. It was a call from my mom.

"Hi, Mom!" I screeched as soon as Bibi pressed the

button on the steering wheel. "We just had lunch and we're heading back to maybe do some painting if we're satisfied with the sketch. Are you at work?"

Before Mom could answer, Bibi interrupted, "Hi, Justine."

"Hi, Roxanne. Sounds like the two of you are having lots of fun."

"We are!" I blurted. "Did you know how to do a dance called the Mashed Potatoes? Because if you don't, I learned last night, so I can teach you. I'm going to download the song to my iPod."

"I only have a few minutes to talk," Mom sort of whispered. "But about Violet staying another week, it's fine with me."

I glanced at Bibi. "Another week?"

"I called your mom last night. Thought we might get down to Laguna Beach and also maybe take a day trip to Santa Barbara on the train. That is, if you want to."

"A real train?" I'd never been on one.

"A real train," Bibi answered.

I grinned. "Yep, I'm staying."

That made Bibi smile, too.

"Okay, it's settled then. I'll call you later, V. Bye, Roxanne," Mom said in her I'm-a-busy-doctor voice.

"Bye!"

I wanted to reach for Bibi's hand to hold it the way I sometimes hold Gam's when it's just the two of us and we're driving and I'm feeling happy. But Bibi had both hands on the wheel, so I didn't.

By the time we got back to the studio, it was hot inside. Bibi turned on the ceiling fan to cool it off, and she was in the middle of teaching me how to copy the sketch to the canvas when she said she needed a nap.

"You sure are a sleepyhead, Bibi."

"I sure am," she replied, rubbing her left arm.

"Does your arm hurt?" I asked as we headed inside.

"Cramps up sometimes when I'm sketching and painting."

"Don't worry about me. I have plenty of stuff to do. Okay if I use your laptop to send some e-mails and pics to Daisy and Athena?"

"Sure, pickle," she said as she logged on for me. "You sure it's okay if I call you pickle?"

"Yep, I like it."

"Okay then, pickle."

37

AHMED'S HOOD
AND MARINA DEL REY

The next morning, I found out two things. The first thing made me smile. We were going to the marina to have lunch at Cousin Lorna and Laura's. And even though I knew they saw me as half white and therefore not exactly black like them, they were still very nice. The second thing—Ahmed was coming, too—made me frown.

His house wasn't too far from Bibi's.

We were walking up to Ahmed's door when he opened it, came out on the porch, and said loudly, "Welcome to my hood!"

A teenage girl standing outside next door asked, "Is that your chick, Ahmed?"

"Naw, it's my cuzzin, nosy."

"I know that's right cuz you ain't never gonna have no chick cute as her."

That made me laugh.

"Shut up, Jo'Nelle!"

"That's about enough," Bibi said, and the nosy girl slinked inside her house.

I glanced over where the girl lived, then at Ahmed in the backseat when we got in the car. "Is that your chick, Ahmed?" I mocked.

"Jo'Nelle? You gotta be kiddin'. She is way too skinny, plus she's not my type."

"What's your type?"

"Not Jo'Nelle. That's my type."

"Can you two please not fuss?" Bibi commanded, then turned on the radio.

Ahmed sneered at me. "We're not fussin'. We're having a friendly conversation."

The next thing he almost whispered. "So what'd you come down here for . . . tryin' to learn to be black?"

"I didn't know it was something you could learn," I told him.

"You're right, it isn't. It's something that you are, all the way down to your soul," he said snidely.

Ahmed Diamond, please disappear.

The twins, Lorna and Laura, lived in a place called the Marina City Club. Their condo was on the seventh floor.

"Hello, hello, hello. C'mon in," one of the twins said as she hugged each of us tightly, then motioned us inside.

Before we could get inside good, the other twin rushed up and hugged us. "Hello, hello, hello. C'mon in." I almost wondered if they'd practiced what to say before we got there.

"They need to wear name tags so we can tell 'em apart," Ahmed whispered, and for the first time I agreed with him.

"Wow!" I said as I made my way to the living room. The ocean view was awesome.

Bibi took my hand and held it. "Pretty amazing, huh?"

I gazed up at her pretty face. "Yep."

"Cooltastic is what I call it," Ahmed said as he scanned the horizon.

"Cooltastic? That's not even a real word," I informed him. "You can't just go around making up words."

Ahmed smirked. "Yes I can and yes I did. *Cool* plus *fantastic* equals *cooltastic*."

He's definitely a being from another planet.

Before long, lunch was ready and we were served all kinds of fancy, unusual foods. Foods from Thailand, India, Africa, and China. "We love to cook," one twin said.

"Just love to cook," the other echoed.

I couldn't imagine one of them without the other. Just like Mom claims identical twins often are, they were *two peas in a pod.*

"A walk around the marina might do us good," the twins suggested after we'd stuffed ourselves.

The marina was one of the prettiest places I'd ever been to. There were all kinds of shops and restaurants and the ocean breeze was just right—not too cold. Bibi was holding my hand, Ahmed was being quiet, and the twins were chatting to each other about their plans for the school year. The diamond ring on Bibi's hand glittered. It felt like I belonged to them. They were mine and I was theirs.

When we reached the big rocks, we sat, watching the rolling waves. Boats, some with sails, raced by and a few people were fishing, but from what I could see, no one was catching anything. From one man's portable radio, jazz music played. The beach sun warmed my skin. Because we looked alike, no one gave us puzzled looks and I remembered my beach dream. Just like the dream, it felt nice.

I glanced around once more at the Diamond family around me, then stood and walked along on the huge boulders toward the deeper part of the ocean.

"You be careful, Violet," Bibi warned.

"I will," I told her.

Of course, Ahmed got up and followed me, pouncing from rock to rock like a cat, showing off.

Finally, I reached the end of the rocks and was admiring the view when I lost my footing. But a hand reached out and saved me from falling—Ahmed's hand.

"Thank you," I told him.

"Ain't nuthin'," he replied.

A selection of homemade desserts awaited us when we got back to the marina condo. Chocolate-filled cream puffs, macaroons, flan, and lemon mousse. The twins really did like to cook and I hoped I'd be invited back again before I went home to Washington.

Even though I was just getting to know my father's family, being here with them made it feel like Moon Lake was very far away—almost as far away as the moon.

38

BRAIDS

Because his dad, Harris, was home when we got to Ahmed's house, we had to go in and visit, and after a while Ahmed and I went outside in his backyard. From across the fence a face popped up. Jo'Nelle again. Her eyes landed on me and she said, "Hey."

"What you want, nosy?" Ahmed asked her.

"Ain't nobody talkin' to you, Ahmed. I was talkin' to your so-called cuzzin."

"Hey," she repeated.

"Hi," I replied.

"Where you from?"

"She's from nunya bizness," Ahmed snapped back.

"I'm from Moon Lake, Washington."

"I'm Jo'Nelle. What's your name?"

"Violet."

Jo'Nelle smirked and muttered, "Huh?"

"Don't play deaf, nosy. You heard her. Her name is Violet. V-I-O-L-E-T," Ahmed spelled out.

"How come your mama gave you a white girl name?"

Ahmed answered for me. "Cuz her mama's white. That's how come."

"For real? So all that hair ain't no weave?"

"Nope, it's not a weave," I said.

"Can I braid it? Pleeeeeeze. I'm gonna be a hairstylist. It'll look good. I promise."

The last time someone had messed with my hair, it had turned out all wrong.

"I dunno how long we'll be here," I replied.

"That you don't need to worry about," Ahmed said. "Once Auntie Roxanne and my daddy start talking, there ain't no stopping them. Plus I heard them say y'all are staying for dinner."

Before I knew it, Jo'Nelle had tossed a bag over the fence and leaped into Ahmed's yard. She sat down behind me and sprayed something into my hair.

"What is that?"

"Stuff for braids. You want cornrows? I could do cornrows real good."

I shrugged. "Okay."

"You'll be sorry," Ahmed warned, and headed inside.

Jo'Nelle must have had some kind of magic in her fingers, because in no time flat it seemed like she was finished. Together we went inside so I could see. My hair was braided into thick cornrows with a side part. And I had to admit, I really liked it. "It looks pretty. Do I have to pay you? Because I didn't bring any money."

"This time it's free, but next time you gotta pay me fifteen dollars."

Because I figured there would never be a next time, I agreed.

Jo'Nelle dragged me by the hand and we burst into the living room, where Harris and Bibi were still yakking.

Bibi's eyes opened wide. "Your hair . . . I love it."

"Sweeeeet," Harris said.

Jo'Nelle beamed. "Told ya. I'm the best. And I could hook you up with some big gold hoop earrings I got a whole mess of."

I fingered the emerald earrings I was wearing.

"No, but thank you," Bibi told her.

From next door a woman yelled, "Jo'Nelle! Get home now! This food's abouta burn up on the stove."

"One other thing. You got that soft hair, so them braids ain't gonna stay that long. If you put rubber bands on the ends, they might keep a little longer."

"Jo'Nelle!" the voice from next door screamed again.

Jo'Nelle flew out the door.

I went into the bathroom, stared into the mirror again, and ran my hands over my braids. I felt like some kind of spice that's only found in faraway places. Exotic, yep, that's the word.

Ahmed peeked in, gawked, said, "Cool," and invited me into his room to play video games.

"So what's your sister like?" he asked as we sat side by side at the computer.

"Daisy? She's mostly nice," I told him.

"She's white, huh? That's what my pops said."

"Yep, she is."

"I think that'd be weird," he said, "having a white sister. Is it?"

Because he'd been mostly annoying, I wasn't sure I wanted to tell him the truth. But he was staring at me with that I'm-waiting-for-a-reply look, and the last thing I wanted was for him to start to badger me the way Yaz does. I hate being badgered.

There was only one honest answer to the question. "Sometimes," I said.

"I figured," he replied, "Because I was thinking about how I would feel and all I could come up with was *strraaange.*"

"Only because some people are stupid and they act funny. That's the part I don't like. But she is nice and kind of cool," I told him. "Mostly I try to think about that."

For once Ahmed was quiet, as if he didn't know what to say.

After too much silence, I told him, "Thanks for not letting me fall into the ocean today."

"Like I told you before . . . ain't nuthin'."

39

THE DREAM BOOK

"What's this?" I asked, handing Bibi a tattered scrapbook the next morning. "I found it in a box in the closet in my room." The words *Dream Book* were peeling from the cover.

"Well, little detective," Bibi joked, "I haven't seen that in so long, I forgot I even had it. That is my mother's Dream Book."

"I expected it to be about dreams, the kind you have when you sleep, but mostly there are just a lot of pictures? Pictures of a washing machine, and a two-story brick house, and nail polish and party dresses, and fancy high heels from a long time ago, and pictures of jewelry. And I found this old hair net."

"Those were my mother's dreams. Things she longed

for. Things lots of colored women who worked in white folks' homes or in the hotels longed for."

"*Colored* means black?"

"It did."

"She didn't have a washing machine?"

"Nope. She used to sneak and do our laundry at the hotel where she worked for what seemed like forever. And she saved her whole life so I could go to college. Saved me from having her life."

"That was nice of her. What was her name?"

"Your great-grandmother was named Madeline Roxanne Keyes."

"So we both have her name."

Bibi's eyes got watery.

"Do you have pictures of her . . . and your father?"

"Of course."

"How come you didn't show them to me?"

She jumped up from where she was reading the newspaper and scurried down the hallway. "Plum forgot!" she said loudly.

I put down the Dream Book, followed behind, and found her standing on a stool in front of her closet. One by one she handed me photo album after photo album, five in all.

"Can we scan these so I can have copies, too? I'd rather do that today than paint. Because I want to know about both parts of my family."

"My scanner is on the blink."

"You should get a new one. They're not that expensive."

"Lord have mercy, you really are as tenacious as your father."

"Which means?"

"Persistent or stubborn."

"Is it a good or a bad thing?" I asked.

"A very good thing if that tenacity helps you accomplish something good," Bibi replied.

I smiled. My word book was going to get full.

Bibi bought a new printer/scanner, photo printer paper, and several flash drives.

"Thank you for bringing me into the new century, Violet. Seems like technology changes every time I blink my eye."

"That's what my poppy thinks, too," I told her.

Right then, I missed Poppy. And as we drove down Crenshaw Boulevard toward home, I suddenly pictured him standing over the stove, stirring and tasting, adding fresh herbs from the garden. Then, like a slide show, pictures of Moon Lake's green pastures and foothills, distant snow-peaked mountains in the winter, and the crystal-clear lake water flashed inside my mind. I could almost smell the pine from the trees.

Violet Diamond is feeling a little homesick again.

40

MY DADDY'S GRAVE

Just when I thought we'd scanned every photo, Bibi would find more, mostly of my dad.

In one of the pictures, he was flying a kite. "That's something I'm no good at, kite flying," I told her.

Bibi chuckled. "Neither was he, but he sure tried. Mostly he liked his books and science. He was a nice child. The best any mother could want."

Because I wanted her to keep on talking about him, I didn't say a word.

"He wasn't perfect, no one is. And like all families, we had our moments, but in my heart, he was simply the best."

It seemed like the right time, so I asked the question I'd been waiting to ask since we were on the plane. "Can we go to the cemetery? I want to see his grave and I want to bring some flowers. Is that okay, or if it's going to make you too sad, we don't have to. But before you say no, you should think about me not ever having a dad and how that makes me feel bad sometimes."

Bibi plopped down in a chair. "He was so excited when your mother got pregnant, V. I'd never heard him happier . . . even painted your room all by himself. *My* Warren would have loved him some you."

"'Loved him some you'?" I'd never heard anyone say that before.

"My mother's country Southern way of saying he would have loved you."

"So, can we please go? I promise not to cry."

"I have a confession to make. I never think about anyone else crying over *my* Warren. I only think about my own tears."

"But he didn't just belong to you, and other people loved him. My mom cries over him, too. And she didn't mean for it to happen. It was an accident."

Bibi rested her head in her hands. Soon her body shook with tears.

"I'm sorry . . . never mind . . . we don't have to go." And then I was crying, too.

Suddenly everything got as still as my house is at two a.m. when I get up to go pee. That still.

Bibi reached for tissues, wiped her tears, and blew her

nose. The next thing I knew, she had picked up her purse and said, "C'mon, Violet."

I trailed her to the door, the sound of the jangling keys in her hand the only sound in the house. "Are we going somewhere?" I asked.

"To the cemetery—he would like that. Funny thing how mothers think no one can love their child as much as they do. Should give me comfort to know that others care. I suppose we were destined, you and I, to have this day."

"Can we bring some flowers?" I asked, eyeing the sunflowers in the courtyard as we stepped outside.

"Of course." Bibi headed back inside, returning with garden clippers and some bright blue ribbon. Before long we had made two bouquets and tied them with the ribbon. "How's that?" she asked.

"Really pretty," I replied as we climbed in the car.

As we drove, something I'd been wondering about got inside my thoughts. "Why is he buried here instead of back near Moon Lake?" I asked.

"I insisted, and under the circumstances, no one opposed me," Bibi replied.

Oh.

And in about forty-five minutes we were driving toward the gates of Forest Lawn Cemetery.

"It hasn't been that long since I've been here, but I always get lost. We'll have to stop at the office."

A nice man in the office went over the map with Bibi and we got back in the car. The cemetery streets winded and curved. Finally we stopped.

We gazed into each other's eyes. "Are you sure?" I asked. "I'm sure."

Hand in hand we climbed the small hill and searched the grave markers until we found it.

WARREN THURGOOD DIAMOND MD
1966–2003
"SIMPLY THE BEST."

"He was," Bibi whispered as she placed the flowers on the grave. "Simply the best."

I kneeled down, ran my fingers over the letters, placed my sunflowers next to Bibi's bunch, and said, "I'm a lot like you."

Bibi pulled me to my feet, wrapped her arms around me, and we stared at the marker for what felt like forever.

Good-bye, Warren Thurgood Diamond.

I hope you're happy up there with the angels.

Bibi sure is nice.

41

THE ROOMS INSIDE A HEART

That night, while Bibi cooked dinner, I called my mom and told her everything that had happened over the past few days, including going to the cemetery and my braids.

"Are you okay, V?" she asked in her mom voice.

"Yep. I saw a lot of pictures today, and Bibi's been telling me a bunch of family history. I'm going to go help her with dinner now. We're making her special-ingredient mashed potatoes."

"That should be fun. You call me if you need to talk. I love you."

"Love you, too. I'll call you tomorrow from the train."

"Promise?"

"Promise. G'night."

"Bibi!" I yelled from the hallway. "I'm going to put on 'Mashed Potato Time' and then I'm coming to help with dinner." She didn't answer. "Bibi?"

The mixer bowl filled with potatoes was going round and round like a carousel, and Bibi was on the floor. I ran to her. "Bibi! What's wrong?" I shook her but she didn't wake up.

Call 911!

"Is she breathing?" the person on the other end asked.

"I think so."

"Is her heart beating?"

"I'm just a kid. Can you just send someone fast to come take care of her?"

"Do you know CPR?"

"I'm eleven years old," I cried.

"Paramedics are on the way. Stay on the phone. Don't hang up."

In a matter of minutes, there was an ambulance outside and paramedics were on the floor beside Bibi. They put a bag over her mouth and started to squeeze it to give her air.

"What's her name?" one asked.

I hugged myself. "Bibi . . . I mean, Roxanne Diamond."

"Is she taking any medications?" one of them asked.

"I don't know . . . she never said."

"How old is she?"

I shrugged.

"Who are you?" another asked.

"Her granddaughter, Violet."

"Do you know where her purse is?"

I ran to the den, and when I came back to the kitchen, they had hooked Bibi up to all kinds of equipment and were giving her electric shocks to try to make her heart start. I knew because I'd seen it in the movies.

They shocked her once, and from what I could tell, nothing happened. They waited and shocked her again. "We have a heartbeat, fellas," one of them calmly said. Then he said something about V-fib and everyone got ready to shock her again.

But a heartbeat, that was good, right?

Another shock was given. A paramedic said something about normal rhythm.

Everything was happening fast. "Is she gonna die?" I asked.

"Dunno . . . Sorry, kid. The rooms inside her heart aren't working right."

"Hearts don't have rooms," I told him.

"They have four chambers," he said. "Two ventricles and two atria . . . four rooms. And when the four rooms aren't working right, you get trouble."

"Is that what's wrong with Bibi?"

He nodded. "Plus, looks like she had a heart attack."

Quickly, they lifted Bibi onto the stretcher. "Where are you taking her?" I asked.

"To the closest hospital with an ICU bed."

"I'm calling my mom," I told one of them.

"Good. Is there a neighbor you can stay with until she gets here?"

"No. My mom's in Washington, near Seattle."

I pressed redial on the phone and Mom picked up. I was spitting out the story when one of the paramedics told me I needed to come with them, but Mom demanded to speak to him.

The paramedic answered some of her questions and then everyone, including me, was out the door. They loaded Bibi in the back of the ambulance and me in the front. Soon the siren was blaring and we were zooming to the hospital. I clutched Bibi's purse to my chest and cried.

I was waiting in a small, cold room near the emergency room when a lady opened the door and came inside. "I'm Ms. Collins, one of the social workers here. Your name is Violet, right?"

"Yes," I replied. The social worker had a worried look on her face.

OH NO!

"Is Bibi dead?" I blurted.

"No . . . but she's in the ICU," Ms. Collins replied. "I know how upsetting this is for you, Violet."

NO YOU DON'T!

She patted my shoulder.

"Can I please see her?"

"Maybe later," the social worker said.

I started crying. "I want my mom," I sniveled.

"I just got off the phone with her. As soon as she can get a flight, she'll be on her way," Ms. Collins said.

The social worker offered me a plastic pack of Kleenex.

"Thank you," I said.

"Are there any family members in the area we can call, Violet?"

"Some cousins." I was still clutching Bibi's purse and I wondered if her cell phone was inside. It's where she usually kept it. I unzipped her purse and rummaged through it. "Found her cell phone," I told Ms. Collins.

"Does it have any ICE numbers?"

"What's that?" I asked her.

"In case of emergency," she explained.

"I don't know."

"Okay if I look at the phone, Violet? Maybe I can find the numbers."

I handed her the phone.

"There's a number for Lorna and Laura Diamond. Do you know them?"

"They're the cousins," I told her.

"That's good," she said, and reached for the door. "I'm going to call them, and I've arranged for the cafeteria to send you some dinner. Are you cold? I'll get you a blanket.

If you need to use the restroom, there's one right outside the door, but promise me you won't wander off."

"Okay."

When the food came, I mostly just picked at it. I really wasn't hungry, and nothing but questions I didn't have answers to filled my mind. Were Lorna and Laura on their way? How long would it take my mom to get here? If she didn't get here tonight, where was I going to sleep? What if Bibi dies? The wall clock said nine thirty. I wrapped the blanket around me, laid my head on the arm of the sofa, and sighed. I needed to see Bibi. I don't usually break promises, but this was one time I had to.

I headed to the door, stuck my head out, and scanned the hallway. At the end of the hall I only saw one person, a man waxing the floors with one of those big, loud machines. His back was to me. Otherwise, the coast was clear. I stepped into the hallway and as quickly as a squirrel scurried in the opposite direction of the man. Where I was, I had no clue. But I did know where I was going, to the ICU.

The hallways were a maze and I took a turn that led me right back to where I started. Now what? I tried it again and wound up standing in front of an elevator. I don't know what most hospitals are like at night, but this one was like a hotel with a lot of vacancies. Suddenly the doors opened and a woman came out. By the way she was dressed, I figured she didn't work there, but I asked anyway, "Do you know where the ICU is? I got lost."

"I just came from there. It's on the third floor. When you get out of the elevator, make a left and follow the yellow line on the floor."

"Thanks."

Like Dorothy on the Yellow Brick Road, I followed the yellow line until I got to the end. The end was a pair of double doors with a buzzer/intercom and a security pad. *Should I press the buzzer?* I wondered. I was just about to do that when I read the notice on the door.

NO ONE UNDER THE AGE OF FOURTEEN ADMITTED WITH-OUT ADULT SUPERVISION.

Fourteen? No way did I look fourteen. I stood on my tiptoes and peeked inside, but I couldn't see anything. Poppy claims every problem has a solution. Hmm . . .

"Are you looking for the ICU waiting room?" A woman asked behind me. I turned and read her name tag. It said NURSE ICU.

Panic. Then I nodded.

She pointed with her finger and said, "Right back there. Follow the green line to the end. And you shouldn't be walking around without your parents," she scolded.

My parents aren't here, I wanted to say, but I figured that would get me into trouble, so I just said, "Thank you," and obeyed NURSE ICU.

Seats lined the waiting room, and almost half of them were filled. Some people's heads were in their hands, others were crying into Kleenex, and four people who seemed to be praying stood huddled together. A man sat alone in one corner, staring at the floor, and in another corner a TV had a picture but no sound. *If Disneyland is the happiest place on Earth, this must be the saddest,* I thought, and sat down in one of the hard black plastic chairs.

I drew my legs up to my chest, hugged them close to me, and put my head down. Nothing bad like this had ever happened to me. Bad sure didn't feel good.

And then—someone said, "Violet."

Lorna and Laura and the social worker were standing in the doorway, and all six of their eyes were on me. I could tell both twins had been crying.

"Lord have mercy . . . we've been looking all over for you!" one of the twins said while the other hurried toward me.

I stood up and she hugged me, not tightly, just warm. And if there is such a thing as a perfect hug, this one was it. "We brought some of your things from Roxanne's house, Violet, and I talked to your mother. She can't get here until early morning. You'll have to spend the night with us." She dug into the tote she was carrying and pulled out my sweater. "Here . . . put this on."

By then the other twin was fussing over me, too, but

Ms. Collins, the social worker, had that look. You know the one. The I'm-mad-at-you-but-I-can't-yell-at-you look.

"Extremely sorry," I told her.

Her lips stayed pursed, but she squinted, and I could tell she was relieved to hand me over to the Diamond twins.

"I want to see Bibi now," I told them once Ms. Collins had left.

"I'm not sure that's a good idea, Violet," one twin told me.

"But it might be her last—" the other one said before she stopped herself.

"My last . . . chance?" I asked. "Is she going to die? Is that what the doctor told you?"

Silence.

Then one twin whispered, "We've already prayed on it."

"God might need her up in heaven," the other added.

"I want to see Bibi now," I repeated.

Bibi was hooked up to all kinds of machines, one that was helping her breathe, and her eyes were taped shut. "Okay if I kiss her?" I asked the nurse.

"Yes, it's okay."

I held Bibi's cold hand in mine and kissed her cheek. I'd just gotten her in my life and it didn't seem fair to take her now. I didn't care if God needed her in heaven, I wanted her here with me on Earth. "I love you, Bibi. I really do."

The twin who was there with me kissed Bibi, too, and we left.

"Our condo in the marina isn't far," one twin said.

"Isn't far," the other echoed.

At their condo I showered, and afterward, like two identical mothers, they tucked me in.

But after they left, I climbed out of bed and did something I had never done before. I got down on my knees and put my hands together. "I know You're up there," I said, "and I know You can hear me. I need You to help the rooms inside Bibi's heart to get better. You already have my dad, so You don't need her, too. But I do. Thank you, please. Amen."

42

WAKE UP

Early morning light shone through the blinds. I opened my eyes.

Where am I?

I fell back to sleep and dreamed that a doorbell rang. "Wake up, Violet," my mother's voice said.

"Not now. Go away, Mom, I'm dreaming," I said.

A hand touched my cheek. "Wake up, V," I heard again. This time it was Daisy's voice.

I opened my eyes all the way. Mom was sitting on the bed beside me and Daisy was behind her. "Is it really you?" I asked.

"Really me, V."

I sprang up out of bed, hugged them tighter than ever, and cried, "Mom! Daisy!"

In the doorway, the Diamond twins watched like spectators.

"The chambers in Bibi's heart aren't working right. You have to fix them," I said.

"I'm a baby doctor, V. I don't think I can fix them."

"You have to try. Please!" I pleaded. "C'mon, we have to go to the hospital." I jumped up out of bed. "Where're my clothes? I gotta get dressed."

I rode in the backseat with Mom and Daisy. "Are you okay?" Mom asked.

"Nope. But if Bibi gets better, I will be," I said, leaning into her. Sitting between Mom and Daisy almost made me think everything was going to be just fine.

As we drove, Daisy ran her fingers over my braids. "They look good, really good," she said, and Mom agreed.

"Thank you," I told them.

At the hospital, because they only allowed two visitors at a time in the ICU, Daisy waited outside with the twins while Mom and I went in.

The first thing I noticed when we got to Bibi's room was the tube to help her breathe was gone. "This is my mom," I told the man who was standing beside Bibi's bed. "And she's a doctor, so you should listen to her."

The man introduced himself. "I'm Dr. Ramirez."

My mom put out her hand for him to shake. "Justine Diamond. I'm a neonatologist . . . in Moon Lake, just outside of Seattle."

They smiled at each other.

"Some very good news," he said. "As you can see, we were able to take her off the respirator very late last night. So, she's breathing well on her own and her pupil reflexes are normal. Oxygen levels are still low, but I'm very optimistic."

Optimistic? That's a good word.

"Thank you, Dr. Ramirez," Mom said.

I kissed Bibi's cheek again. "Wake up, Bibi," I told her, watching her eyes. Nothing. "What do we do now?" I asked my mom.

"We wait."

"She's off the respirator," Mom told the twins and Daisy as we left the ICU.

Lorna and Laura squeezed each other's hands, uttered "Praise the Lord" at the same time, and went inside.

Because it was such a sad place, I didn't want to go to the ICU waiting room, but that's where we headed. Can you guess who else was there? Victoria, Harris, and Ahmed Diamond.

While my mom, Daisy, and the Diamonds got acquainted, I talked to Ahmed. "She's breathing by herself now, not with a machine," I told him.

"Now that's cooltastic news, real cooltastic news," he said.

Cooltastic. I was starting to like that word.

Every now and then, we checked on Bibi to see if

anything had changed, but by noon nothing had. We were heading to the cafeteria to have lunch when Ms. Collins, the social worker from yesterday, showed up.

She ignored everyone and made a beeline to Ahmed's mom, Victoria, and stuck out her hand. "So nice to meet you, Dr. Diamond. I'm Ms. Collins, we spoke yesterday," she said.

Victoria smiled and shook her hand. "Pleased to meet you, but I'm not Dr. Diamond. She's—"

Before she could finish, Ahmed pointed at my mom. "She's Dr. Diamond."

Ms. Collins's face got that I'm-so-embarrassed-I-wish-I-could-evaporate look. "Oh . . . I'm so sorry," she said.

"No problem," Mom told her as she put one arm around my shoulder and reached out her other hand to Ms. Collins. "Thank you for looking after Violet."

Ms. Collins took out some cards and handed one to my mom. "If there's anything I can do to be of further assistance, please feel free to call." Then she handed a card to Ahmed's mother. "You too, Mrs. . . . ?"

"Diamond," Victoria replied as she reached for the card.

Harris spoke up and extended his hand for Ms. Collins to shake. "And I'm Harris Diamond."

Ahmed chuckled. "We're all Diamonds, can't ya tell?"

"Of course," Ms Collins said, then added, "I sincerely hope Mrs. Diamond will fully recuperate. Nice meeting everyone."

"Nice meeting you, too," the Diamonds echoed.

The cafeteria food wasn't bad, or maybe it just tasted good because I hadn't really eaten since yesterday and now that we had good news, I pigged out. Mom, Daisy, and the rest of the Diamonds seemed to like one another.

It feels like a family.

Lunch was over and back to the sad waiting area we went. We'd only been there for a few minutes when one of the ICU nurses came and asked us to come into the ICU.

"What happened?" I asked.

"She's awake."

As soon as the nurse opened the ICU door, we disobeyed the hospital rules and all rushed inside. Before the nurse could stop us, we were in Bibi's room. She still had oxygen things in her nose, but her eyes were open. I took her hand and she squeezed it. She cleared her throat and tried to talk but could only whisper.

"Easy now," the nurse who was at her bedside told her, then frowned as she reminded us, "Visitor policy is two at a time."

"Just for a minute?" Mom asked.

The nurse nodded. "Okay, Dr. Diamond. But just for a minute."

Bibi glanced around until her eyes finally landed on Daisy.

"That's my sister, Daisy," I told her. "Daisy Diamond."

"Daisy? Warren sure loved him some you. Like a

daughter, he told me," Bibi said in a low, raspy voice, and reached out her other hand to Daisy.

Daisy took Bibi's hand and replied, "And he was my daddy."

Next, Mom took Bibi's hand in hers and held it gently.

Just like real diamonds, the people surrounding Bibi's bed came in many colors. And one by one Bibi admired their faces, smiled, and briefly held their hands.

Ahmed's words from earlier rang in my brain. *We're all Diamonds.*

43

A TEMPORARY GOOD-BYE

We stayed in Los Angeles until the day Bibi got out of the hospital. She'd had a pacemaker and defibrillator put in to fix her heart, and the twins had moved into Bibi's house for a while to be her nurses. I still didn't want to leave, and I begged my mom, but she had to get back to work and said the twins had enough to do, watching over Bibi.

Mom and Daisy were saying their good-byes to Bibi, but I stood alone in the hallway outside her bedroom, my back against the wall, trying hard not to cry, wondering how long it would be until I saw her again.

Mom called my name. "Violet?"

"Yep," I answered.

"Bibi wants to see you," Mom said.

I stepped into the doorway. Mom and Daisy were standing at Bibi's bedside and one of the twins was sitting in a chair, reading what looked like a Bible. Bibi was propped up in bed with pillows. All eyes were on me.

"Can Bibi and I be alone?" I asked.

"Of course," my mom replied.

"Yes," the twin said.

When we were alone, I went in and sat beside her. After a couple of washings, my braids had come out and my curls were back. Vases filled with flowers were everywhere and the room smelled like perfume. "How are you feeling, Bibi?"

Bibi caressed my hair. "Better and better," she replied, then rested her hand on mine. "I've been waiting for us to have this time alone to thank you."

"Thank me for what?"

"If you hadn't been here and called 911, I probably would have died that day. You saved my life, Violet."

So much had happened, I hadn't even thought about that. And instead of crying my eyes out the way I thought I would, instead, I grinned. "I did, huh?"

"You did. And because you did, you and I will have lots more fun times together," she said softly.

"When?"

"Your mother said you can come visit for a week at Christmas."

I frowned. "Christmas? That's a long time from now."

"And if the doctors say it's okay, she has invited me to go to the mountain cabin with your family this August."

Our week in the mountains—I'd forgotten all about that. Knowing I was going to see her soon made me smile again. "Wow! That'll be absolutely awesome."

"Yes, absolutely awesome," Bibi agreed as she pulled me to her, hugged me gently, and kissed my forehead. "I love you, Violet."

I kissed her cheek and took a deep breath, trying to memorize her sweet smell. "Love you, too, Bibi. And as soon as I get home, I'll call you."

"You promise?" she asked.

"I promise."

Before long, Daisy, Mom, and I were at the airport, thanking Harris, who had driven us there, and saying good-bye to Ahmed, who'd come along.

"Later, V," he said.

I couldn't believe it, but I actually felt a little sad. "Later, Ahmed."

"So, cuzzin . . . you ever gonna get to come back to LA?" he asked.

"For a week at Christmas," I replied. "Is that great?"

"Cooltastic!" he said, and we laughed and waved good-bye.

44

BACK TO MOON LAKE

After Poppy and Gam had picked us up from the Seattle airport, we'd all gone to have dinner. From the way they were treating me, you would have thought I'd been gone a whole year.

Being missed feels amazing.

As usual, the drive from Seattle to Moon Lake put me to sleep.

I'd be lying if I said it didn't feel good to be home, in my own bed, cuddling Hazel. The past weeks had been like being in a washing machine, whirled around and tumbled. So much had transpired. I like the word *transpired*.

Gam cracked my bedroom door open. "You asleep?" she asked.

"Not," I replied as I sat up in bed and turned on my lava lamp.

Gam sat in the chair by my bed, and it felt good to have her there. My gam.

"Seems to me you had quite an adventure, Violet Diamond," she said with a smile.

I laughed. "Boy, did I."

Gam patted my head. "But you're okay?"

"Better than okay," I told her.

"Not so many missing pieces, huh?"

I thought about the question for a while and replied, "Hardly any."

"For that and for having you home, I am happy." Gam kissed the top of my head. "Good night, V. I'll see you in the morning. Love you."

"Good night, Gam. Love you, too."

Right then, for the first time ever, Gam felt like she was all mine.

Before I could turn off the light, Daisy peeked in. She was wearing a dress and tall platform shoes. "Where're you going?" I asked.

"Out with Wyatt."

Of course.

Her hair was pinned up in the back in a way that made her look older than seventeen.

"What do you call that hairstyle?" I asked.

"A French twist. You like, *ma petite mademoiselle?*"

"It makes you look older." I climbed out of bed and touched the pearly thing that was stuck in her hair. "What's this thing?"

"A French comb. I could do yours. It would look cute, V."

"With my big ears? I don't think so."

"Your ears aren't big, Violet. I've told you that a million times."

"They're bigger than yours and Mom's."

Daisy laughed. "Everyone's ears are bigger than mine and Mom's. Mine are so small, I'm surprised I can hear out of them."

"Did you know big ears are prized in some cultures?" I informed her.

"No," she replied.

"They are," I said, and I fingered the lobe of my ear. I'd forgotten to take out my earrings, the emerald studs Bibi had given me. "I can't believe she gave me real emeralds. If you ever want to wear them, you can, okay?"

Daisy smiled. "Thank you, li'l sis." Daisy's face turned serious and she stared into my eyes. "You seem happier. Are you?"

"Yep."

"Cool. Very cool. *Je t'aime,* V."

I'd heard that enough times to know that meant "I love you." *"Je t'aime,"* I replied.

Daisy patted my head and left.

Nothing about us being different mattered right then, nothing.

We're like any other sisters.

45

VIOLET THE DIAMOND

The next morning, Poppy was in the kitchen as usual. Bacon was frying on the stove. "Eggs and bacon coming right up," he said.

"I was wishing for eggs and bacon just a few minutes ago," I told him.

"Still wishing, huh?" Poppy asked.

"Wishes are okay, but they're for stuff that's not serious. For serious things, prayers are better."

"You learned that in your travels, I presume?" Poppy asked as he whisked the eggs.

"And other things," I told him.

"Like?"

I glanced over at his cookbooks. "Like how to make

grits pie, and short ribs, and Bibi's special-ingredient mashed potatoes. I can even teach you."

"I'd like that," Poppy said, and he broke out into a huge smile. "Nice to have you home, V."

After breakfast, because I was a little tired, I lounged around the house in my pajamas. Mom and Daisy had gone to work and Poppy was practicing on his putting green. "Want to go to the golf course with me?" he asked.

I shook my head. "Maybe tomorrow."

From upstairs, I heard Gam on the phone, working. *Nothing has really changed,* I thought, *except me.*

Lots of stuff was whirling around in my brain. Maybe, like Bibi said, I would be a writer someday. I pictured myself in a room filled with books, all written by me, Violet Diamond. And I'd travel all over the world and become a bohemian and have an exciting life. Thinking about that made me smile.

I headed to my room with Hazel, who refused to leave my side and mewed loudly every time I put her down. "Spoiled kitty," I said.

After I plopped into bed, I stared at the ceiling, picturing the candles glowing on the birthday cake Bibi had bought me. I remembered placing sunflowers on my daddy's grave, dancing the Mashed Potatoes, and listening to Nina Simone. I thought about the trip to Hollywood, the orchestra of wind chimes, sitting around the table enjoying the noisy Diamond Family Feast, Ahmed reaching out and saving me from falling into the water, and the twins, Lorna and Laura, talking like an echo. I hoped being with them was going to become a *usually always* thing. And though I was glad to be back in Moon Lake, I missed Bibi. I looked forward to seeing her soon and promised myself to call her tonight.

And as I nodded off into a nap, the sound of the door-bell and loud knocking startled me, and the next thing I knew, Athena was standing in my doorway. Early this morning, she'd called and said she'd be over around two because she had to go with her mom and grandma to Dio's doctor's appointment. I glanced at my clock. It was eleven thirty, still morning.

She held out her arms like a superstar. "I'm here," she proclaimed. "His appointment got canceled until tomorrow."

I bolted up out of bed and we hugged.

"Thank you for being back!" Athena said, and plopped down. "The summer was only getting worse and worse without you. My grandma's still making me cook all day and Dio is still getting every ounce of attention from my parents. It's like I disappeared. I'm still here, I kept telling them, but they didn't hear me—or at least they pretended not to. I've gone from being the one and only family star to being nobody. Dio, Dio, Dio. That's all I hear, morning, noon, and night." Athena finally took a deep breath and asked two questions. "What was it like? Did you have a good time?"

Ponder, that's a word I like, and it's what I needed to do before I could answer her. I didn't know where to start. There was so much to tell her.

Athena didn't wait for an answer. "You look the same . . . Do you feel the same? I mean, now that you met your other family."

"I still feel like me . . . only more," I told her.

"More?" she asked.

"More me." There was really no other way to explain it.

When I think about it, it's an odd name, Violet Diamond—almost antonyms—a tiny, delicate flower versus the hardest mineral on Earth. Mostly I've been like a violet, small and shy, but lately I'd begun to feel like a diamond. It was as if the sparkly part of me was growing inside. I liked the way it felt and hoped it would stay there forever.

Finally, my name, Violet Diamond, was beginning to fit me.

"Are you glad to be home?"

"Yep, but my wanderlust is worse than ever now," I replied.

"What's that?"

"A desire to travel around and see every part of the world."

"When we grow up, that's exactly what we'll do, promise?"

"Promise," I said.

"Did you meet any famous people in Hollywood?" she asked.

"Not," I replied.

"For real?" Athena frowned.

"Hey, want to go ice skating?" I asked her.

"Are you kidding? Anything is better than what I've been doing the past couple of weeks."

I went to my door and yelled out, "Poppy! Can you take us to the rink?"

ACKNOWLEDGMENTS

I offer great thanks to Nancy Paulsen for her editorial guidance, alliance, and insight. I also extend many thanks to Penguin Young Readers Group for their continued support of my writing. To my children and grandchildren, thank you for being the luminous pieces in my puzzle of life. As always, I thank the Great and Holy Spirit for gently guiding me along this Earthly path. Love and kindness are essential in these times.

brenda woods was born in Cincinnati, Ohio, raised in Southern California, and attended California State University, Northridge. She is the award-winning author of several books for young readers: Coretta Scott King Honor winner *The Red Rose Box*, *Saint Louis Armstrong Beach* (on eight state award lists), *VOYA* Top Shelf Fiction selection *Emako Blue*, *My Name Is Sally Little Song* (on four state award lists), and *A Star on the Hollywood Walk of Fame* (Golden Sower Award finalist). Her numerous awards and honors include the Judy Lopez Memorial Award, FOCAL Award, Pen Center USA's Literary Award finalist, IRA Children's Choice Young Adult Fiction Award, and ALA Quick Pick. She is an avid reader, has two sons, and lives in the Los Angeles area.

Visit her at www.brendawoods.net.